Published by Jaded Ibis Press, *sustainable literature by digital means*™ an imprint of Jaded Ibis Productions, LLC, Seattle, Washington USA.

Cover art by Christian Duran.

THE Nowhere MAN

a novel by

Marlon L. Fick

Jaded Ibis Press
sustainable literature by digital means™
an imprint of Jaded Ibis Productions
Seattle • Hong Kong • Boston

~ In Memoriam ~

Sophía Renee Chavez Fick
(2002 – 2002)

Laura Chavez Fick
(1959 – 2006)

Contents

Francisco Segovia's Preface

Bolivar Collins died alone, a traitor to God and Country, hardly a worthy subject for a book. A few weeks after his death, Ms. Regier Toulet informed me that a large box would be arriving within the week. She instructed me to sort through the material and inventory its contents. The only thing I knew of his life was the same as anyone else who would have read about him in the news—he was a traitor. The FBI wanted him for reasons beyond his treason, reasons that are still unclear. His first book was a best seller that was later banned by many libraries and all good Christian schools—although the ban had more to do with the author than the book. The work itself, entitled *Winter Signs,* was not particularly immoral—indeed its protagonist was a missionary who took the printing press westward during the Jackson years, the 1820's and '30s. Later, many argued that the book was immoral because its author was anti-Christian and anti-American. Truth be known, not many Americans ever knew the author and no first hand accounts of him exist, much like his namesake, Simón Bolívar. It is safe to surmise that Bolivar Collins had little in common with the clean, moral character that his first novel projected. That is, it did not follow the predictable pattern of first novels, which tend to be biographical. As for his last and final disappearance, there is only speculation. Americans felt compelled to invent possible scenarios to explain what no one could confirm: 1) He had returned to Havana, where he died (which I am persuaded to believe is what most likely occurred) 2) that he lived out the rest of his years in México, 3) that he had been sent by the Cubans to one of our Holy Wars in the Middle East to interfere with our efforts there. The most twisted of all the accounts was one that insisted he was not anti-American, nor even anti-Christian; it was simply that circumstances had placed him at the wrong place at the wrong time. This last view—generally believed by his admirers—holds that he was kidnapped by a Mexican drug cartel.

I went to work the day the box arrived and found their contents appalling. Leafing through his diaries, I found a litany of a life of a wretched debauchee. The boxes contained his diaries and manuscripts, dozens of inane articles, unopened fan mail, mostly from morally questionable women, signed editions by other authors with his undecipherable marginalia, and a photo of Collins beside the tyrant Fidel Castro and a negro woman with two little girls.

After perusing the contents of these boxes, I went to see the Chief Editor, Ms. Regier. I reported to her precisely what I have just made public here. As always, Ms. Regier's dog, Orkle, was asleep by her desk, and as always, Orkle woke up, raised his head and growled at me, baring his fangs.

To which, Ms. Regier always added her the comment, "He doesn't like you, Segovia. I'm sorry."

My distaste for the task befallen me was based on the simple grounds of universal morality. She simply told me to go back to work or find a new job.

"Go back to work, Segovia."

Orkle growled whenever she used my name. A beast of a dog, nasty and brutish. A Labrador of some sort. Yellow. With the same green eyes and same yellow hair as Ms. Regier, though I am quite certain that the dog's fur was its natural color. While some claim this breed to be exceptionally friendly, I never saw it. And he followed Ms. Regier everywhere so I was cursed to work in a hostile environment where both of them bared their fangs at me.

Ms. Regier informed me that not only would it be my job to oversee the inventory, but that once we had finished we would edit the diaries in such a way as to give the public a more accurate accounting of his life—that is, more accurate, she believed, than what was then already widely believed or invented in the press. The point was moot since the authorities had already banned Collins. I protested anyway. I said,

"I prefer not to," I said, and, "There is nothing socially redeemable about the man or his diaries."

To which she said, "It is not important that a book be moral, only that it be a good book."

I did consider writing a letter to the authorities and testifying to her defiance, but I let it go. I said,

"I do not understand how it is possible for a good book to be good if it is not moral."

To which she replied, "It is in fact immoral to write a bad book, so it will be up to you to make sure that it is not a bad book. As to the morality or lack therein of Bolivar Collins, I couldn't care less. Now then, as a consolation, if it is a consolation, you have a choice. You may write the preface to his diaries, and should you choose this option, you may say whatever you wish, or you can resign now."

Upon reading this, you have realized that I chose the first option, for which I ask your forgiveness in the name of God and our Blessed Flag. I had little choice. Having not enough money saved to sustain a prolonged search for a new position, I was obliged to agree to the task of cobbling together the stuff of his worthless remains.

Strangely, when I turned to leave her office, she added,

"Segovia . . ."

Orkle growled.

"Yes, Ms. Regier?"

"I knew him."

"Oh?"

"Yes Segovia . . . and you will never know how much you owe the man."

Orkle growled.

"That is all you need to know for now, except you may use the working title, *Philosophers in Love,* until I've decided on the best title for the book."

Then she paused a moment and added, "I was aware of what your response would be; in fact, I was counting on it. And would you, on your way out, tell my secretary that I would like some chai. Then please ask her to pick up my daughter at school, but first see if she can get Karli on the telephone to translate for her mother. I want to see if the two of them will write a piece that I can include with the material, something like a postscript, something that will give us all a sense of closure to all this nonsense, even if it is a futile wish."

I never understood that comment, "I was counting on it," and I confess that I still do not. Counting on my having an aversion remains a mystery.

With the box came new horrors and enigmas, as if demons had scrambled a dozen jigsaw puzzles and left it there, flying back to Hell, laughing all the way. Still, it was difficult not to speculate on the purpose of the thing in question.

In the box I found items I could but barely comprehend and which obviously could not be accounted for by his diaries: a gold wedding band on a chain, a rosary together with a photograph of Castro, the negress with the little girls, and the author. In the same box we found three bullets, which were 45/70 in caliber, large enough to bring down an elephant or a bear. The bullets were resting in the toe of a sock.

There were cloves woven into a necklace; a small, wooden crucifix; and a chicken foot with green, blue, and yellow feathers tied around it with leather cord; and a matchbook with the number 7 written on the inside flap.

I have chosen not to list the patently offensive objects. I will, however, share mention of one final thing that I found objectionable, as long as we are not presenting the image, as such: It was a rolled up painting on canvas which revealed, in stark realism, the figure of Bolivar Collins naked and hanging from a cross, with a naive, Rousseau-like jungle painted in the background. In attendance is what appears to be a group of soldiers. The body of Collins is hideously disfigured beyond the wounds one might expect from a crucifixion, and his nakedness grotesque.

At last, before this story begins, I would conclude with a prayer that this story be lost for eternity for fear that some unsuspecting innocent find it and, quite by accident, allow the reading of it to invite the devil into his soul. If this manuscript should fall into your hand, reader, it is advisable to burn it without reading beyond this introduction.

In concluding the preface to the diaries of Bolivar Collins, I would simply and humbly inform readers of my own biographical details. My name is Francisco Segovia, or Francisco Emilio Sagrado Corazon de Jesus Segovia, and my friends call me "Paco." I come from a well-born family in Jlalpan, Querétaro, in the country of México. Jlalpan is a modest town. I was born on March 9th, in the year of Our Lord 1990, a Holy Roman and Apostolic Catholic. Upon graduation from High School, I served honorably in the United States Army in Afghanistan and received my discharge only after being wounded in that conflict. I should add, I enjoy joint citizenship in both The United States and México. I returned to México after my discharge, and I enrolled in the National Autonomous University in México City. Ultimately, I chose a career in journalism and served as an apprentice at one of the local newspapers, *Diario*, or "Daily." A year after my practicum, I received an offer from my current employer to be one of the copy editors for the bilingual Spanish/English division. The Chief Editor, Ms. Regier, then contacted me in México to solicit my employment here in New York, though she never liked me from the start and I have never known why.

The Posthumous Memoirs
of
Bolivar Collins

~ 1 ~

The Apology

I have made a great many mistakes in my life. I have known success, but for all my mistakes, my victories have been pyrrhic. St. Augustine never squandered his sins. He let them illuminate a path to God, but I wasted mine. I wallowed in them, allowing ideas and places to replace people, killing the potential wholesome life of the body by carnal means, until I was as Shakespeare wrote, "a walking shadow." Had my name not become infamous, I would be content to let the past be the past. Should this—what this is, I am not sure—should this *whatever* come to light, I wish it to be known that it has become clear to me now. I have learned this through my daughters, especially my youngest, Karli, who taught me not to be afraid anymore of the horror of existence. As I watch her grow, I confess, I see in her the object of what I, myself, could never become, except for the blessing of being a husband and father, which is all I desire to be known for. As to whether my story comes into public view, I leave that to her better judgment, a judgment that despite her young age is superior to mine. And I leave it, too, to the wishes of my wife. Should they decide not to release these pages, then they will simply stand as my confession and my apology for the wretched life I led those years before I knew my wife and before Karli was born. However, if this story should become public, then I wish it to be known—despite persistent theological doubts that haunt me—that I left the world a believer, or, at least, one who wished to believe. I cannot say that I believe in angels, at least not in the way that my wife believes, but when our daughter was born, she smiled at me after only moments in this world. She smiled. It was only a moment, but in those seconds I believed that her smile was the reason why I was put on this earth. I believed forgiveness was possible.

1976 was the 200th anniversary of the United States of America: The Bicentennial. I was a boy in St. Louis, Missouri—a stupid boy, as in "foolish," but book-smart to a fault. The farther my reach extended into the flat world of books, the more detached I became. I could not see into the hearts of people. I was simply a frightened child. I think my sister Sherry tried to tell me that one Sunday afternoon after an unfortunate event which coincided with Easter that year.

~ 2 ~

Sunday Morning

"I raise my Ebenezer to God! Raise it to God!" I kept hearing him say. His voice echoed in the sanctuary even after the faithful departed, and it continues to haunt me. But other events, earlier, the night before and into the morning blended together in a night and day without sleep. . . . *if you don't think, you won't exist . . . don't think . . . just go . . . walk the line . . . walk along the outer banks without looking back, for if you look back you will see you have left no prints . . . There is a light. A very small light. There are moments as supernumerous as the sand that slips through your fingers until you are old. Every grain, every atom of myself should understand itself in relation to others, but they don't. The monad is indivisible, therefore a ghost, therefore it knows its role in the cosmos, its holy spirit, and how it is destined to interact with the infinity of all other monads that constitute existence.*

Leibniz was wrong—or, he was not right for me. None of the atoms ("monads" he called them) belonging to me has even the slightest awareness of her, if I can even remember her name . . . *Micki?* That's a boy's name. Micki Seaton said,

—An erection for the resurrection.

or some crass thing as I lost my virginity in the predawn hours of Easter Sunday morning. And,

—You really don't need the rubber because my Easter eggs are worthless.

The car windows frosted as she moaned into an abyss from which I never returned. Something of a Venus of Willendorf, she reminded me of a pale, fat, dopey bird that I saw in a book about the birds of Africa. Large breasts that hung low from sheer weight, large boned, pallid, grey skin in moonlight, the dirty end-of-winter Micki with hair the color of dust, sitting in her cotton, extra-large grandma underwear up around her oversized hips

—So . . . what do you think? [She asked.]

As for that, I sat there in my own underwear, size normal, and thought of something I could say that would sound very nice. She was twenty-two or twenty-three, just back from college to teach me things that in retrospect I wasn't ready to learn. I had just turned sixteen, acne'd and unpopular at school. *You are supposed to say something nice*, I thought:

—That was . . . amazing.

And I supposed it was. But I think I was more upset than amazed.

—I took an Art History course this semester? [She said.]

Micki had an awful habit of raising her voice at the end of her phrases even when not posing a question, as if all affirmative statements were questions. It was annoying. I wanted to say to her,

—There is a glimmer of glamour in grammar, and that goes double for intonation.

It's true: The Latin word for *grammar* is cousin to the word *glamour.*

—And [she said] there is this statue called "Adonis," and you look like him.

—Really, I've never seen a Greek statue with pimples.

—Only his hair was . . . you know . . . the color of marble?

I looked briefly at her eyes to see if I could find my reflection.

—He must have had hair like yours. [She said.]

—Actually, the Greeks painted their statues. Probably his hair was black.

—You sure know a lot for a high school kid.

—I've only read about it.

—Whatever . . . You're hot.

Then I found my reflection in her eyes. I did not think I looked like Adonis. I could see that I had pimples. I wouldn't have cared much about it if my father hadn't insisted on weekly trips to the dermatologist for lancing and large doses of ineffectual antibiotics that weakened my immune system and made me susceptible to a variety of much greater infirmities later in life, like malaria, typhoid, dengue fever, and yellow fever.

A few hours later I was sitting beside my sister, staring up at the empty cross hanging from two wires over the altar at the First Baptist Church and trying to avoid Micki's furtive glances from the other side of the aisle. I wanted to get lost in the woods, wanted to just leap the back pew, jump in my Pontiac and head for the woods, away from the suburbs. The pastor was thrusting with his finger at the empty tomb, like a hollow Easter egg, just a shell. He is not here! He is not here!

The walking dead. Maybe that's what I am. I've left no tracks, or I've covered them so well I remain a mystery, though not a divine mystery.

Suddenly I was aware that all of us were standing to sing because Baptists like to sing, and on Easter, every year, they sing "Christ the Lord is Risen Today..." And... when "He" returns, the pastor said, He will separate the sheep from the goats. Which one was I? Which was Micki? I probably never understood a sermon to save me as well as I grasped enormous tomes of philosophy.

Leaving the church, ubiquitous daffodils were thrusting out of the ground, blasting their yellow trumpets. Redbuds were turning to purple haze. In a few days, the tulips would probably open their lips and expose their stamens, then the dogwoods, followed by magnolias. These would have been signs for the reading, had I, at that time, read anything other than books. They were probably warnings of some awful tragedy disguised in natural beauty, flowering crabapple trees so intensely red they seemed to be in agony, dead bulbs laid to rest in little graves, dead all winter, then the weather goes wild in the apocalypse of electric storms, until, when it is over, the sun comes out and the people wander out of their suburban homes bedizened in the sun too bright to see.

After Easter service I went to the bluffs to look at the Mississippi valley and think. I drove to Missouri Bluffs, first stopping at home to pick up Birdie, my dog, a bluetick coonhound and boon companion. She hopped up onto the passenger side and faced forward. From behind, another driver might have mistaken us for man and wife. If she had not been a dog, or I had not been a boy, we might very well have been man and wife. We knew each other's habits in detail. Sympathized. Found deep and abiding companionship in each other. She was, though, over-protective of me. She could, and had on occasion, snarled and snapped at anyone who tried to get close to me, with the exception of my sister, Sherry. Sherry could walk right by her nose, exposing her ankles, and Birdie would let her pass.

If she could have spoken rather than howled up at the trees, our conversations might have been matter of fact.

—Why don't you ever take me hunting?
—You know I don't like guns.
—I'll tree them, you shoot them. It's all I want. Please?

22.

—Can't you content yourself with dog food?

—Come on. It's not about dog food. It's about the thrill of the chase.

—So, go chase.

—What? And leave you alone by your little twig fire?

I had built a small fire from twigs and spread out a green, wool army blanket to rest on.

—It's okay, really. Go chase. I'm sleepy anyway.

—You're upset about something.

—Yes. Maybe. A little.

—Then I am, too.

—What for?

—For you.

I felt like crying and didn't know why. Soon I fell asleep and slept through the afternoon until a voice woke me. The fire left a small grey circle of ashes. Birdie was curled up in a ball, but the voice woke her too. It was my sister.

—You awake?

—How did you find me here?

—I brought you here two years ago when I got my car. You don't remember? Anyway, I had a pretty good idea this is where you'd be.

—I needed to think.

—No book today?

Birdie got up, yawned once, stretched, and wagged one time for Sherry.

—It was a long night last night. Too sleepy to read.

—I saw you were the first to leave. You missed the Easter egg hunt. When Birdie wasn't at home, I figured you'd come out here.

—They aren't worried or anything…

—Mom and Dad? Ha. Mom's already passed out and Dad went straight to his lab, or supposedly the lab, after service. Peave came by to see if you were home.

Peave was a short and pudgy neighbor kid whose father was a member of the Mafia, or so it was rumored. He was a tag-along little chum who would do anything I told him to do: eat a tadpole or a worm. Peave was innocence incarnate, someone else I would never be able to protect.

Sherry was the closest person to an adult that I knew. I didn't know my brother Charles very well. After six years away in Vietnam, he came back in 1970, married a Catholic girl on the south side, and barely ventured out to visit us, except for the obligatory Christmas and Thanksgiving.

—Last year, Charles came at Easter. [I said.] He didn't come this year.

—Charles is Charles. It isn't anything against you. He doesn't want to deal anymore with Mom and Dad.

—Oh.

Sherry put on her sweatshirt. It was still chilly. She looked down at the Missouri River, far down below the bluffs, winding around to meet up with the Mississippi and disappear in the south. She said,

—You know, I'm going to college in a few months.

—I know.

—California is a long way from here.

—I know. I sort of know.

—It's just been the two of us for a long time now.

—Yeah.

—You used to sleepwalk a lot and crawl into my bed and wake up crying.

—I guess I remember that.

—It's just… I'm not going to be here to protect you.

—I understand.

—No you don't. You don't understand that I'm just a kid, too. All this time, I've just been a kid. I don't know any other way I could have raised you.

—I'm okay. Please, don't worry over it.

—Bolivar, I love you. You're my baby brother.

—I love you, too. More than Mom, even.

—Try not to hate them, Bolivar.

—It's a whole two months before you graduate. That's a lot.

—You promise to come out to California if I can't come home right away to St. Louis?

—I promise. Can I bring Peave?

—Do you have a choice?

We laughed.

My other companion was a thin fellow named Dennis. Dennis was a young Werther, Goethe's Werther. He pined and planned. Planned and pined, never happy with reality as reality was, so he was always projecting ideals. Peave lived in utter misery at home with a family far more dysfunctional than my own, but always projected the moment we were in as extreme blissfulness. There was nothing ever better than right now. We were an odd threesome that made no sense.

After my sister's graduation, there was a small ceremony on the lawn behind the estate. A lot of her friends and teachers were there to shake her hand for being Valedictorian. Dad made me put Birdie in a cage so she wouldn't bite anyone. My mother mixed martinis on the deck and my father bragged about Monsanto projects to my sister's science teacher, an attractive older woman, who seemed interested in "dioxin." Sherry was pretty busy to notice me, so I stuck my fingers through the chain-link fence of Birdie's cage and told her I was sorry to put her in jail and asked her to kiss me.

A week later my sister was gone. She didn't stay for the summer of 1976.

She was gone in her little Ford Pinto. And my compass and direction were gone, too. All she left was her empty bed with its bright yellow bedspread and frilly pillows heaped with stuffed bears that wore ridiculous fake smiles. I didn't see her again for thirty years. She held me and whispered in my ear to be good, and then she was gone.

~ 3 ~

from **The Road Home**

a fragment

I'm standing beside a highway in Nevada. There is a car in the distance. At first it seems to be moving slowly, then a little faster, and then suddenly it roars past me at 80 or 100 miles per hour. When I look again I can see my sister's face, briefly. Then it disappears.

~ 4 ~

Jewish Girlfriends and

The Ethics of Spinoza

Lullay, Thou little child,
Bye bye, lullay,
Bye bye

Michelle Kerson invited me to her room where she told me we had a little less than an hour before her mother would be home with the groceries. We were standing in the kitchen and Michelle's hair was tousled in back. I looked at the floor with my hands in my pockets while her mother put away the groceries and asked me diffident questions, like whether I had picked out a university yet. I rummaged in my mind through the first nineteen of Spinoza's axioms, trying to find one to hang onto. Trapped in a corner of the kitchen and hearing questions aimed at me, which Michelle answered, it struck me that I was standing in Spinoza's greatest paradigm of all: Total freedom from total determination. The novice first encounters the notion that everything is already determined and it appears to be that way in the works of Spinoza, but the totality of his worldview expresses a kind of determinism that extinguishes itself in the freedom of totality. I wanted to vanish into freedom. Take Birdie and just disappear like an old mountain man of the past.

Michelle was good at acting like she had not just fucked a guy in her bedroom while I was trying to maneuver to the door on the other side of her mother. Mom and daughter had black hair and green eyes. They both moved like cats. Michelle caressed a strand of her hair over her right ear and her mother put some frozen vegetables in the freezer with the same nonchalance.

Her mother kept asking me the requisite questions and Michelle advocated for the defense.

—He still has two years to decide where to study, but he's leaning toward NYU or Wash. U.

—. . .

—His parents are both from good families.

—. . .

—His dad is a chemist or scientist of some sort. He developed a defoliant at Monsanto that helped the soldiers out in Vietnam by clearing the jungle.

—. . .

—He's in the school choir, that's how we met.

—. . .

—Yes, he does lots of other stuff—like the football team and track in the spring.

—. . .

—Well of course he hated Nixon! What do you think?

It went on like that while I stood there searching for an exit strategy.

—No, they're not Jewish, but his family doesn't mind as long as we just remain friends.

I don't remember how I escaped. I don't even remember seeing Michelle after that. Spring vacation came a day or so later and I spent the week at the Baptist retreat, on a lake in Illinois, where I met Nancy White, who was about twenty-one, and her older brother, who looked a lot like Cat Stevens. I liked her instantly and even felt little pangs of love. Somehow I managed to convince myself that this was the girl for me. It didn't matter that she was engaged to a gas station attendant. Nor did it matter that Jesus seemed to affect her the way marijuana did. To obtain my goal, I pretended to love Jesus intensely. She ignited the innermost core of my world, so it was easy to simulate the appropriate degree of reverence and awe, or religious emotionalism, for the one and only savior. I sported a cross, one actually given to me by Micki, inscribed for my birthday, and "Easter, 1976." Nancy wasn't exactly expecting me to barge in on her plans. A day after I met her, I left the lake front retreat grounds, where my tent was pitched near the circle and where everyone gathered to pray to a wooden cross, build a campfire, sing hippie praise songs. I showed up at her house, unannounced. She was in the bathroom getting ready to go out with her fiancé. I waited for her in her backyard. When she came out, I professed my adoration and love and put her in the difficult situation of having to tell me she was engaged. None of that matters now. I spent that night on her brother's couch chain smoking and drinking. Her brother, the Cat Stevens look-a-like, waited until I was sufficiently over the edge, offered me a little tab of Purple Microdot, and went for me when he was sure I was sufficiently elsewhere. The rest is purple haze, but the next day I thought, okay, good, I am a hundred percent certain that I prefer girls to boys.

As for visions, I wasn't sure. Of course, I never said anything to anyone, especially to Cat Steven's sister, Nancy, who the next night, probably out of curiosity or pity, accepted my offer to picnic by the lake. Nancy's hair was brown and wavy like the ripples on the muddy lake. She had a small chin and a soft, faint mustache growing from the corners of her mouth. By degrees, and cautiously, I worked to put her at ease. The wine helped, which I poured in remembrance of Jesus.

I think of the poet Wang Wei and the Taoists, climbing up a mountain to look into the distances, and not the distances of longing or endless desire, but the blank spaces of space itself, out of which, somehow from this kind of contemplation there would emerge a sense of union with the cosmos. The abyss is not just an abyss, but also an UR-nothingness full of the infinite possibility of existence. I was thinking about Wang Wei and exploring her body when it occurred to me as we kissed that the Chinese practice of eating lotus blossoms made absolute sense. Strangely, the ecstatic mingling of Jesus, wood smoke, wine, and Wang Wei opened in me some portal into a different consciousness, and Nancy White was the vessel, the vortex through which the physical world and the uncontrollable current of my mind mushroomed in outer space. This worldly being, the sensuous and fleshy details, is a conduit to something transcendent.

~ 5 ~

Dostoevsky's Sexual Politics

The early summer of '76 was spent reading Dostoevsky. "I am a hateful man. I am a hateful, spiteful man," I loved repeating, with my teeth clenched. Yes, indeed, there was supposed to have been some way out of the abyss, but I hadn't the foggiest notion by what path, though I drove my Pontiac, a classic, at insanely high speeds along the Missouri bottoms in search of the way. Sometimes Dennis and Peave rode along—pessimist, optimist, and undecided, with undecided at the wheel. Sometimes we turned the Zeppelin to full volume, filled the tank with airplane fuel and the inside of the car with the brownish green smoke of Acapulco Red, strapped on our football helmets, and raced a train to the crossing. I never let Birdie go on these excursions as I considered them to be slightly dangerous.

About that time, another schoolfellow, Jesse, entrusted me with his Camaro, and, as it turns out, his Camaro came with his girlfriend, Sally. The Camaro was red and Sally was an Ozarky redneck blond who had heard of London and thought it was a country, but she was somewhat pretty. Slight overbite, but pretty, and I liked that I could see her pelvic bones protrude between her elastic halter-top and her low riding jeans.

Jesse wasn't sad to be mustering out without his car and without Sally, but it bugged him that 'Nam was over and he might not get to kill anyone. He was really a nice guy who dwelled on how he longed for battle. He graduated with D's and went off to the army with dreams of being in the 101st, and then the Rangers. He referred to Jimmy Carter as a peace loving liberal prick pussy who would only delay our ultimate showdown with the Reds. Then he was gone, mustered out, and I had Sally. He wasn't gone more than a day and a night when Sally, the Camaro, and I were parked at Broken Heart Lake. She had a gallon of Boon's Farm strawberry wine and was twisting off the aluminum top just as I finished starting our campfire. I told Birdie to roam the woods, and I spread out a green army blanket from the army surplus store. There just wasn't room enough in the Camaro, unlike my Pontiac; in fact, driving down, Birdie had to straddle the gearshift.

It struck me how backward she was when she insisted that Blue Oyster Cult and REO Speed Wagon were the alpha and omega of "music." Birdie yawned at her opinions. The Rolling Stones were too sophisticated? (That's a paraphrase. She didn't actually know the word *sophisticated*.) I didn't care. I let her play her boyfriend's 8 tracks and when I saw her gulping the Boone's Farm like soda pop, I knew that she'd be gagging soon, and heaving. She threw off her jean jacket and one sleeve landed in the fire. The heavy metal added a certain mood of raw emergency and an exciting, imaginary violence to the ordeal. The next day I had teeth marks, hickeys, and scratches. Proud of my battle scars, I hummed to myself, in my mind, "I am a hateful, spiteful man."

Then Sally was no more. It's not as if I killed her and dumped her body in the lake. Practically the opposite. We stopped when she started vomiting. In the morning, I was putting dry twigs on the fire to re-kindle it when Sally woke up. All she said was "gimme the keys." She looked like Death. Sin or Death. Her hangover weakened her enough to allow remorse to seep in. I gave her the keys and that is the last I ever saw of the Camaro. But it was still '76, the anniversary of freedom and unadulterated sexual liberty for all, so I did not take the loss of the new Camaro very hard.

It doesn't matter if I don't think. If I don't think, I don't exist. If I no longer cry, then no one will notice. I will be just fine. If I do not exist except as a will-o'-the-wisp in the mist, I will be fine.

Birdie came to back to the campsite. I was skipping stones, getting about six, seven hops out of some of the better flat rocks.

—Hey, Birdie. Catch anything?

—Nothing. But you look worse for the wear. What happened here last night?

She found the source and started sniffing, then lapping Sally's Boone's Farm vomit off a large flat rock.

—What are you doing? That's disgusting!

—No it isn't. It's delicious.

—That could make you sick!

—How would you know? Ever tried it?

—Yuck!

She went back to lapping. Then stopped. Looked around.

—Where's Camaro Girl? And where's the Camaro?

—Gone.

—How we gonna get back home?

—Hoof it, I guess.

—You mean go by paws.

—Yeah. Gosh, I'm really sorry.

—I don't get it. She was really into you.

—For a while.

—You okay?

—Yeah.

—Liar.

—You want to swim or anything? You could use a bath.

—So could you.

~ 6 ~

Chamfort's Aside

I finally understood Chamfort. There's no language, no words, none of the nonsense of making sense in the ethereal zones outside time. The vortex of woman, death, and religion as oneness made sense. The moment apart, like an aside, played on the dice of a girl's spine, made sense. How we came together made sense. I wanted just one of them to be the first and last woman. It is all I really ever wanted, and it was never to be. The one woman. First indivisible being. The Platonic reunion with my other half. Actually, that may have been Aeschylus—of myself with myself, or herself with myself as oneself.

> *The first girl I made love to*
> *held me too hard around the neck and cried.*
> *She shook when she cried and her breasts trembled.*

> *Wanting her had something to do*
> *with the first family*

> *and letting go of the past, the mirrored arcades*
> *with their columns of rain—*
> *my thoughts rush after her and pool in self love.*

The past is present. The tangled
sheets turn on themselves.

I wander as if missing in passages
through her body, through the open doors
and empty rooms and subways, finding her
caught in branches of rain
and the webs of memory echoing in the subterranean,
finding, for once, the smothered cry I couldn't
dig from it's trench, or return from the well.

I travel through her
wondering if I am dust
or if she is, dust and darkness of a thousand years ago,
its song of opalescence
showering down in the sexual ether.

I fling myself,
scatter myself on broken stones
beside her, joined like two stones joined
to make one arch,
one tributary moment, infinitely receding, opening, vanishing . . .

Time outside of time, there she is, like the object of a religion, the beads twisting between my fingers. Woman is the portentous Non-Being and in the most sexual moment-non-moment not one article of clothing need be removed. After I knew this, I was sure the sun would never rise again, proving that Bertrand Russell was right regarding problems of certainty. In its place, a flaming cross rose over the eastern horizon as I tried to remember what did not take place in time or on earth. I felt a more intense desire in the absence of "other" than in the presence. Chamfort knew this. He was, unfortunately overshadowed by his contemporary, Descartes. There is no desire outside time, no achingly long distances, no woods lovely, dark and deep, no magic alchemy of the elemental. There was no desire, no distance, hence no measure of time or space between us.

I was a teenage disaster of epic proportion. The work of imagination, very lofty books, a tempest of hormones combined to douse the prospect of ever growing up. Yet, Chamfort had prepared me for Schopenhauer's discussion of free will, leading to a logical, but ridiculous conclusion, that all out abstinence was the only way to true freedom.

~ 7 ~

A Dialogue on *The Golden Bough*

The last year of high school, I became even less social with people, the keepers of the Clock, and I took to the woods with Birdie more often. One of my book companions that year was Sir James Frazier's abridged *The Golden Bough*, which I only checked out because T.S. Eliot's poetry was incomprehensible without it.

—What are you reading now? [Birdie asked.]

—Do you think the earth is female?

—Probably, yes.

—Wouldn't it be both or neither?

—Hello? I'm a dog. Your logic is a little over my head. So what's it about?

—Well, it talks here about the Earth Goddess: The fertile earth, the receiver of sun and rain, was deemed, by the collective imagination, across many cultures at many times, female. Coatlicue, the Earth Goddess of México, becomes the Mother of Jesus—that simply wouldn't fly at First Baptist, but there she is, poised as the Virgin, riding the foam and spray on her shell-like surfboard. The Spanish/Mexican painters still paint her conch, her vulva, as if it were a nimbus, a surrounding light, but it's helpful to remember that it was and IS an impenetrable shell. The human notion that the earth is gendered is quaint, but a baseless fancy.

Birdie agreed, probably just to avoid an argument. For that, for her, I never liked the word *bitch,* or rather I thought it terribly unfair to give a pejorative twist to a word that should have been sacred. The same goes for the word *squaw* . . . .

Squaw, Birdie, beloved, wherever you are.

~ 8 ~

Kant and Female Sexuality

Is there anything redeemable in the mafioso with such a crooning voice as Sinatra's? Or Nietzsche, for that matter, even if he did not intend for his work to fall into the hands of the Nazis? I didn't know my intentions at all. Was I therefore evil? Perhaps I was. My preacher said I was (said all of us were) born stained. The great German opera star, Elisabeth Schwarzkopf, barred from ever singing at Carnegie Hall, sinned by virtue of marrying a high-ranking official of the SS. So perhaps I was also beyond all redemption.

I wondered if Frank Sinatra, with his sweet mafioso voice, had ever read Nietzsche. I think all music is great, but crooning was not part of my generation, screaming was. So it was odd when this very well carved Italian statue of a girl, call her the Fedora Girl, started hanging out with me. Actually her name was Janet Orrico. Close cut black curls, a fedora, and horned rim glasses. Under that was soft plushy, unblemished overly white skin. She said "No" a lot, but each time she said "No," and I stopped, as I am somewhat of a gentleman, she asked why I was stopping. Confound it. All right then, don't stop. Then she started screaming. That was something new. "Are you all right? Do you want to stop?" No! No! I whispered that it would be better to say "Yes," if she meant yes, and in this way, we might better communicate, but I was talking across three decades. How had a young girl in the '70s so absorbed the culture of the '40s? "No means Yes," she said, and I said, "Say yes, okay?" (What is this? Some perversion of the negative dialectic?) Before it was over, smoke came out of my ears trying to walk the tight rope of paradox, the No and the Yes. She seemed thoroughly satisfied, whereas I felt like I'd just been through an obstacle course of interpretation. I turned to Emmanuel Kant the next day, with the consolation that, although difficult, a philosopher says exactly what he means. This of course makes the philosopher difficult to understand, but in a manner unlike girls.

Birdie saddled over next to me.

—Whatcha reading now?

—Kant.

—What for?

—To clear my head.

—Why don't you just take me hunting?

—Later, okay?

Girls remain enigmatic. Girls are not sisters. Rather a riddle. Unstable mass. Metallic rock floating through the void. I feel as if I am nothing more than a space probe reaching out . . .

Start first with The Prolegomena. *The Foundation for Any Future Metaphysics.* Then the Critiques. After school, I went to work. After work, I read Kant, a meticulous little man who obsessed over the subject-object paradigm and tried to employ both an empirical and rational approach, one that would bring Platonic and Aristotelian philosophy to bear on the problems of epistemology, metaphysics, and ethics. Until I knew that anal sex was even possible, I was befuddled by his "posterior analytics" and I read on, under the mistaken idea, that "a priori," meant coming too soon. Still, in some sense, a sexual act at some level must exist as an idea, whether a priori or a posteriori, outside of direct experience. These days were before someone invented the Dummy books. Had there been a dummy book for Kant, I would have cheated. Wittgenstein, who arrogantly proclaimed that he'd never read any philosophy, had heard of something of this wonder boy, and summed it up, "The goal of zee philosophy vaz to show zee fly za vay out of zee fly glass—until I, Ludwig, arrived."

I think Wittgenstein considered Kant his own personal fly.

The Fedora girl was truly a frustration. She may have been the one who turned me into the pitiful fly and doomed me to crash over and over against the invisible wall forever. She could not even achieve "satisfaction," as Mick Jagger put it, if Sinatra wasn't playing in the background. Background? No, foreground. No, Sinatra. No, foreplay, the act, and the afterglow all in one. This kid is sixteen and can't get it on without the pop king of the '50s? I already knew that my conquests were driven out of terror of being thought of as an insecure nerd, but in Fedora Girl, I had met my match. Nerd in the old sense as in *autistic*. She was, which I didn't know existed then, one in twenty or thirty, who loves to accept your hard work and skillful tactics, but has no notion of Subject/Object reciprocity. Nothing was Kantian about her. I was supposed to be the Subject and She was suppose to be the Object. Or, conversely, some may reason. Maybe the Subject and Object never "come" together, but, in the ideal, *a priori synthetic*, the object is already given unto the subject. Perhaps if Fedora Girl had read Kant, she might have applied his categorical imperative and quit just lying there every time, saying No for Yes, a test of the negative dialectic like the emergency broadcasting system. You have been experiencing a test. Should it have been an actual emergency . . . but no, to you this is just a test of the "no" and the "yes."

~ 9 ~

Visions of Excess

"You can visit but you can't leave." That's a great sentence for starting any ghost story. It also applies to the time in which we live, regardless of the century. I believe the German philosopher of history, von Ranke, would concur. Despite the swoosh of world events, reality and the fiction we make of reality are whizzing by. I stood by on the side of a road somewhere in Nevada, in the desert that is me, and felt nothing. I remember seeing my sister drive away in a 1976 Ford Pinto, Robert Kennedy assassinated, I watched Vietnam on TV and wondered every night if that was Charles ducking for cover in the background, and I remember the day we lined up at the airport to welcome him home and how he walked right passed us, like he didn't know us anymore, and how I started a list of things I wanted to take to Switzerland with me when they came for me, but they never came, the Body Snatchers, like they did for my brother Charles. Then there was the trampoline act on the moon, The Nuclear Threat, The Chicago Riots, The D.C. Riots, The Florida Riots, The Mass Suicide in Guiana, Manson and Dahmer, Apartheid, President Reagan, Elvis faking his death and sneaking off to Canada to hide, Genocide, 9/11, the Oil Wars, and even the antichrist in the White House proclaiming the end of History and Environmental Protection. Everything seemed to happen *out there* while I grew old, staring out at deserts in Nevada—as for that, deserts all over the world.   I wasn't exactly absent. In fact, by my late twenties I had seen more of the horrific side of humanity than most would probably witness first hand were they to live to be a hundred. My life took me everywhere: Europe, Africa, The Middle East, Central and South America . . . I'd seen starvation and war, squalor, even murder. What could my sordid adolescence amount to other than a minor series of mistakes, compared to a major series of mistakes which constitutes the natural trial and error of basic evolution.

Sex doesn't make any sense, but oddly, making whoopee is an occasional reprieve from senselessness, paradoxically the supreme act of senselessness. For a little while I simply pretended that some girl made sense, and then she was gone. They approached me like cars on a desert highway. They seemed to be moving slowly. Then they roared past at 90 or 110 mph and disappeared over the curve of the earth.

~ 10 ~

Plato v. Pythia

Heraclitus claimed that we may never set foot in a river at the same place. Plato's theory of forms, however, insinuates an achievable ideal as well as the accursed burden of perfection, which, while we may never realize it, exists in the absolute, and so plagues us with an impossible standard, a miserable cross to bear to Calvary. Armed with Plato, I toyed with the idea that there was One girl for me somewhere. Anyone who really knows the theory of forms knows I'm making a mockery of Platonic theory—I'm sorry—but then so did Christianity, which adopted the Only One notion from the Greeks and the Hebrews (who somehow got the idea from India, and from whence Mesopotamia encountered the idea), and who were chewing that over daily in cities like Corinth and Ephesus. Well, as a Baptist I can claim to have inherited many such misreadings with virtually executive privilege: translations of translations, in addition to agenda-laden interpretations. As a Baptist and of course as a kid, I was free to pick and choose whatever scripture served my shortsighted ends. Add Plato to the mix and somewhere out there was the perfect girl, with the perfect form, a Sati for my Shiva, a balance—the girl from whom all blessings flow. The original. I need only climb the mountain and consult the Pythia. The Pythia, a prophetess at Delphi, sat in her temple at Delphi and breathed an intoxicating smoke all day long, so she was probably quite stoned. There was a lot of that in my time, adding to or detracting from the act of interpretation, depending on one's fractal point of view.

~ 11 ~

The Cartesian Meditations

I don't think, therefore I do not exist. The first holiday away from college, Thanksgiving, I drove to St. Louis to see Birdie, who was staying with my brother, Charles. Charles put up with Birdie. Or she put up with him. Though she was never allowed to go free after that and was condemned to the concentration camp of a fenced backyard. Birdie was, at that time, the only female who made sense to me. I was one with her. Her earthly form as a hunting dog made no difference to me. It was not a perverted love, either; rather a pure and unadulterated man/woman union, much like the male and female union between a nun and Jesus when they mate for life.

When I saw her again, she became hysterical and jumped on me, yelping,

—Where have you been! You bastard! Oh I am happy! Happy! Happy!
—I'm sorry. I tried to explain it to you. I have to be in College. It's something people do.
—Never mind that you . . . You! Just pet me!

With regard to Cartesian meditations, we are all searching for ground zero, a place to begin. If Descartes' maxim, "I think, therefore I am," were true, then it served to reason that inverse was also true. I could simply not think, and whatever I did wouldn't matter, since I didn't exist. Then the drastic pressures of political and social reality pull us out of the solipsist's cave and force us into pragmatic discourse. Such was the case with the events surrounding my beloved Birdie, whom my brother, Charles, referred to as a "bitch" because, he said, that is what you call a female canine.

I have always detested the word *bitch*, given that it is used pejoratively and is terribly unfair to female dogs. I find it miraculous that a single female can have one litter of progeny by as many as three male dogs. The female dog deserves reverence and respect.

Charles put Birdie to sleep. I was away at school in a dorm when he paid someone to murder her. So I did not speak to him for about twenty-five years. It might have been longer.

~ 12 ~

The Symposium

This must have been about the time that Jesse got his wish. A circular from our high school reported that he had been killed in the line of duty. It was an odd bit of information since we were not at war, but it was later revealed to me by members of the American Communist Party that he was ambushed in El Salvador where he had been sent to train death squads. News from that part of the world, by the time it reached the United States, was scant, twisted, and mostly censored, so the truth about Jesse may never be known. As for me, I was still living life pretty much as I had all along, unescorted and untutored in the ways of actual people.

A classmate poked his head into my dorm room and asked if I wanted to go protest.

—Sure. Protest what? [I asked.]

He wasn't sure. Either we were going to march against U.S. support of the militarists in El Salvador with the campus Communists, or we were going to meet up with a larger group protesting the university's investments in South African gold, hence in apartheid. Either way, the FBI filmed us from the upper windows of the Admin Building, which was neat.

I walked along in the crowd, raising my fist, trying to feel angry. A woman, with grey hair and flat teeth, spoke to me:

—I've seen you at these things.

This was impossible, but I lied,

—Yeah, I think I've seen you too.

She—Maude?—had on a jean jacket over a white t-shirt with no bra. She said,

—I also heard you talking about Marx at the Catfish.

This may have been true. I went there often with other philosophy students and drank until tricked into believing that I understood ideas which I really didn't—these occasions were usually on Friday nights since I took school somewhat seriously. But the drinking age was 18 then and didn't turn to 21 until I turned 21, so it's possible the old hag had listened to us drink and argue.

—Are you a Marxist? [She asked.]
—Well... Yes, but minus the material dialectic part, which is based on a pretty faulty 19th century premise, grafting the Natural Sciences onto the Social Sciences, because I don't think we can do that.

I could see she didn't understand a word I said. What she was really driving at was, "Are you sexually liberated," which a lot of hippies (old and young) confused as a Marxist idea, when actually the idea is more easily traced back to first century Christian Orphic cults, and later, romantic poets and theorists like Percy Bysshe Shelley and Byron.

She had to have been old before hippies arrived on the scene. She was just shy of being the age of my maternal grandmother, though she had managed to keep a shadow of her figure. The popular film, *Harold and Maude*, was not released until a year later. Had I seen it before, maybe I could have dealt with the situation better. When I arrived, I smelled a sickening sweet incense mixed with cat shit and curry simmering in the kitchen. Dinner conversation was unfocused. I remember she said,

—I was at Woodstock.

And me thinking, *So you were the oldest person at Woodstock*. I asked,

—You really think Ronald Reagan has a chance?
—No, how could he? He's an actor, and a very bad one at that.

A black light illuminated her silver pubic hair. All the way back I kept thinking, *Birdie, Birdie, Birdie, lovely limbed and waggy, sweet, innocent Birdie . . . I was lost in you . . . lost . . . and reality found me again.* In a man/dog relationship there is the proper mix of the rational and the mystical, the earthly and the sublime, the total reciprocity that makes gender itself irrelevant. In the old hippie—Maude, was it?—I'd found stark naked reality punching me in the stomach. I was walking so fast that the cat shit and curry, and cheap wine made me stop, green and sweating despite the cold of November, and I vomited beside a tree, wiped my mouth with my sleeve. The bell tower donged twelve times. The throb of every dong resonated through the woods and down the grassy hill into the stadium where it was caught and slung back so its echoes crowded against the next blow of the hour.

~ 13 ~

The Sirens of Karl Marx

or

How I Did or Did Not Become

A Communist

Before leaving for Africa, I had just one more year to decide where to step in Heraclitus' river, the river that is never the same. Chaos everywhere.

> *Or when the rain is falling,*
> *when it is filling the banks of the Congo,*
> *we made love to each other . . .*
>
> *When the rain falls on rusty pylons, opaque screens*
> *and dilapidated shacks,*
> *on scrawny tin shops and overturned bins,*
>
> *and the boarded horizons*
> *we look to remember,*

when it falls on the signs
to illuminate the words,

how shall we read them?
As dead languages?
The names of the dead?

All meaning washed clean
and buried in mass graves?
Sealed hermetically,
undisclosed
as a wound cries out its own absence?

Or shall we imagine
the meaning
passing as the echo of thunder into other meanings
as transparent,
as elusive
as the wing of a fly?

I circled around the rim of the earth six times and bounced off, desperately grasping the edge of the flat earth in what seemed like its final seconds.

I remembered my Marxist friend was having a party. I hadn't seen Rodger Bland much since Maude and the rally against U.S. aggression in El Salvador, but only recently had bumped into him at a bar called the Catfish where he was having a beer with his girlfriend, Ellen. He asked if I was "ready to join the party, yet."

—I'm thinking on it.

—Actions are better. Hey, we're having a little party after graduation night. You're welcome to come.

—I'm Bolivar.

—Ellen. Nice to meet you.

—Thanks, Rodger. Ellen, will you be going?

—I don't like crowds and I also have to finish a project.

Ellen was an architecture student. They worked those poor students unmercifully. I said no to the party but I had the address in my wallet and something made me change my mind. It was an accident or a whim that changed whatever destiny there was.

It was at Rodger's house. I arrived at 9 o'clock. No party. There was a meeting. There were people of all sorts: Africans, Asians, Middle Easterners, local workers. It was an open house for foreign students who belonged also to the party. The other party, the fun kind of party, wasn't to start until all the business was concluded. The meeting was sponsored by the Kansas Chapter of the American Communist Party, Rodger presiding. All so serious! Like German philosophy. I wondered if anyone there even knew how to throw a proper party, although I did see a keg in the kitchen as I'd come in. How very dry! It must have started long before I arrived because a couple of members were nodding to sleep in the back. Anyway, I noticed a skinny girl in drab green pants and a green t-shirt chain-smoking Marlboros on the front row. Her hair was the color of dirty sand. She'd spoken twice between 9 and 10, something or other "radical" about the slowness of farmers in Kansas to organize and I noticed that she had a southern drawl. I wanted to meet her. Rodger had finished the agenda items and had moved on to "new business," and "new members," at which time I didn't think beyond *I want to meet this girl* and I stood up and said, I'd like to join the party.

Sometime after the keg was tapped, and the Communists had begun to loosen up a bit, I stepped out on the back porch where Sarah McBride was sucking on a Marlboro. Less than a half an hour later, she led me to an upstairs bedroom with serious intentions in the party way. There were but one or two glitches in the plan. First, the party per se was crowded with all manner of people, Muslims from Africa, Communists from the United States, musicians whose affiliations blew with the current winds, and wannabe scholars from countries I had barely heard of. Mid- . . . mid the natural act, the bedroom door swung open. A large woman began yelling in Pashto and then switched into English, staring down on us in the intense bare light of interrogation.

—Where is Rashid? [She said.] Rashid is here? What are you doing? Where is Rashid!

Skinny McBride fell silent and inert beneath me. I managed a yelp,

—OUT! GET OUT! JESUS! GET OUT!

After what seemed like a long time, the Afghani woman gave up her hope of finding her husband cheating in our bed and turned and left, leaving the door wide open. So I got up and slammed it and flipped back off the light. The whole thing was daunting. Finally, Skinny McBride broke the ice with some oh-my-goodness-like-comment until we were both back into the grove of the same purpose. Minutes later, we were both about to achieve orgasm when Rodger swung open the door to the room, which in all fairness, was, in fact, his room, and said, "Oops, sorry," and closed it—which forced Sarah McBride and me to once again regress back into talking. That is when I learned that she was a very intelligent girl who had grown up pretty poor, the daughter of trade unionists in Arkansas. Then there was moonlight in the room, enough to capture her smile and a rare look of human warmth in her eyes.

The morning light and the smell of coffee woke me up. Sarah's side of the bed was empty. Rodger was reading a book on the adjacent single bed.

—Oh. Um. Sorry. [I said.]

—No problem. My roommate is out of town. You want some coffee?

—Yes, I think I do.

My head was throbbing.

—What are you reading?

—Georg Lukács.

Rodger was incapable of giving the short answer if asked, but I risked it—that or I am reducing our conversation down to a manageable size for the sake of paper or memory. I asked,

—In summary, it is about . . . ?

—Art and Literature. Art and Lit that does not directly benefit society, unlike Gorky, for instance, is reprehensible and decadent. The function of art is to advance the cause of inevitable revolution . . .

The bright light coming into the room at a sharp angle suddenly darkened Rodger's prescription lenses.

— . . . it is not to indulge petty, self-serving interests that serve no one.

—What of one's natural desire to express oneself freely?

—Ah! [Rodger said.] You have fallen prey to the romantic myth of the individual, the "cult" of the individual. But no one exists apart from the body politic.

—Sure. I grant that. But no ideology can stamp out the virtual universe that exists autonomously in a single person—unless by murder.

—We [by which Rodger meant "We Communists"] are not suppressing anyone's individuality; on the contrary, we liberate them from their oppression, make them understand their importance.

—You almost sound like Jesus.

—Pish!

—Think about it. You want to reach out to the poor, the oppressed, but it's a call for war. The difference is that Jesus reached out to the poor and dismissed the self-righteous rich, or "the upper classes" as you call them: Matthew, chapter 10, verse 13. Peter was a tax collector, the equivalent of an extortionist in those times.

My early youth, spent as a Baptist, slipped out quite unintentionally, as I have never been prone to quoting chapter and verse. Rodger replied,

—Religion has done nothing more than indoctrinate people into believing their lot in life has already been cast, and that there is nothing they can do about it but be happy in the weird idea that God shines on them for being miserable.

—It's too early in the morning for this.

—It's past eleven.

—If your ideology is ultra anything, you probably don't get much of anything.

But Rodger had a characteristically automated come-back.

—That's just word play. In the real world all true thought is methodical and follows a methodology.

—Rodger, I'm seeing circles. It's probably from the beer last night. Is there any more coffee?

—Yes, I'll get you some.

—No. I'll get it. Thanks.

~ 14 ~

The Party Way

If M has a desire for X, then if X occurs, M will be pleased. The rationalist lives in a comfortable world reducible to logical formulae. Replace M with myself. If I want . . . say, the skinny blue-eyed she-comrade, and she complies, or X occurs, I'll be pleased. Test the formula.

I was pleased. Sarah wasn't gone forever. She called me that afternoon and we continued to see each other. Test the formula. Although I've never bought into the "material dialectic" of "history," viewing it as a 19th century obsession to make all things conform to the Natural Sciences, I placated my friend and allowed him to sign me up, and I got the girl to boot. Rodger and I became boon companions, loving to disagree on just about everything. I paid my membership dues, attended the meetings, listened to long boring lectures, and learned to address the other members as "Comrade."

The bland world of simple logical maneuvers, the reducible world of X is Y, or History as a series of dialectically determined events, giving rise to revolution until we have progressed beyond classism, is, to be circular, bland, as bland as everyone wearing the same clothing and sporting the same little red star. But anyone can get beyond these details. I liked Rodger, liked his girlfriend Ellen, who, as it turns out, wouldn't have anything to do with his politics, and most of all, I liked Sarah McBride enough to lie to her and tell her that her poems were very nice—thinking, how can a really smart girl like this write such drivel?

It must have been a month, maybe two after X occurred, that is, after I found my she-comrade at the Party's "party." After Rodger slammed down his gavel like Lenin, for the last time, I was thinking . . . *If M believes that doing C either will lead to S or has some considerable likelihood of leading to S, then if C is within his power, this belief will add to the probability of his trying to do C.* I stood on the back porch thinking . . . adding to the probability of C . . . if I were to kiss her, she would be more likely to kiss me back, despite her political seriousness for yet a more serious form of communing.

Rodger left for El Salvador to work with the trade unionists and the farmers. He was a true believer and I admired him for actually following his convictions with actions. No one here knew how many people the Junta was murdering. Few knew that the leaders of the Junta, members of their death squads, had received their training near Fort Benning, Georgia, at The School of the Americas. Fewer still knew that the Junta was fully backed and funded by Uncle Sam. All we did know, after Rodger left, was that Ellen was pregnant and I was pretty sure that Rodger didn't know about it.

A note came to me from Rodger's sister. All it said was that he had been killed by the army in El Salvador. Oscar Romero was assassinated a few months later. But the full impact of these events was beyond my grasp. I simply felt ashamed.

When his sister's note came, I took it to Ellen's apartment. She would have married Rodger if Rodger had shared even a small part of his commitment with her. Ellen put the letter on the kitchen table and made a pot of tea. I noticed how well her philodendron and jade plants were doing.

—They aren't mine. [She said.] Nothing here belongs to me.

Nothing here belongs to me . . . If the Marxists could only cut their so-called science with a bit of the existential, then maybe I could believe in something.

Ellen only meant that she was taking care of the apartment for a professor who'd gone to Morocco on a sabbatical.

—You know, he read around ten different newspapers a day. [She said.]

I knew he read a lot of newspapers. He was one of the few people who read more than I did.

—That was finally what clinched it. There just wasn't anything left for me. I mean . . . .

She couldn't finish her sentence. She was crying. Then we were quiet. Then I asked,

—Did you know that he wrote very nice poems?
—No. [She said, astonished; very nice poems would require feeling in concert with his intellect.]
—They're pretty good. I have some. Would you like me to bring them?
—I don't even fucking care.

But she did care, very much.

I didn't really know if I knew how Ellen felt, but the day we received news about Rodger, my sister informed me that Charles had put Birdie "to sleep"—a nonsensical euphemism for death. Perhaps I was unable to let go or grieve properly. I never exchanged so much as a word with another dog for many years.

. . . finally the sky is burning . . . the hay bales bear themselves like golden bells in the light, and wind that bucks a hedgerow wallows in a rise . . . finally the sky is on fire . . .

~ 15 ~

Russian Polarities

I started reading Roman Jakobson, the Russian linguist—and often I went to check on Ellen, sometimes with Sarah along. I was so captivated by his studies of aphasia and his daring analogies to the polarities of language and metaphor, that I instantly became a Russian Formalist—in spirit. The most wonderful thing about Jakobson is not his genius for the theoretical, but his subversion. In Russia, in the '20s, there could be no "speculation." Even our understanding of the arts must be grounded in proven scientific facts. So the formalists struck back with a vengeance, couching their wild leaps and pirouettes in language laden with scientific lingo. The bipolarity of the human brain is manifest in the horizontal and vertical poles of language itself. Simple observations about how metaphors work along these two poles, as contiguous and comparative, reveal this truth. The great minds, after the revolution, had a choice: either they could pretend to be scientific and elude the authorities, or they could die in Siberia. Sarah McBride, like Rodger, had very little tolerance for deviance from the established order of the material dialectic. She sensed my deviations. As I noted, she wasn't at all stupid, not in the slightest. Jakobson and, later, comments I made about "the autonomy of a poetic text . . ." precipitated our premature withdrawal from each other.

~ 16 ~

The Idiot with an Open Mind

C.S. Lewis warned against pluralism: "An open mind in questions that are not ultimate, is useful. But an open mind about foundations, either theoretical or practical, is idiocy. If a man's mind is open on these things, let his mouth at least be shut." What looming language. I cower to think that I ravel away my story like a Penelope, waiting for her man to come home, redundant and obtuse, without a single cornerstone, no foundation whatever, no ultimate cause or willingness to proclaim an ultimate judgment—save maybe a word or two from one's sister.

It'll be or not be—that is the question, and there is probably nothing less noble. My failure in a nutshell is that I let a life of plurality choose me, as I'm incapable of making any judgments on my own. So we are left with something like Saint Augustine's confessions, without the conversion and salvation, and without the sainthood. Lewis is of course referring to moral paradigms, while I haven't any to refer to, and so instead, my reading of Lewis' warning is twisted to my whims. Still, he did say, "Pluralism is useful," though I doubt he meant the word as it applies to sexual appetite. By the time I arrived in Africa, I was already aware of my life as a directionless quest, less like the noble and most excellent adventures of Cervantes' great *Don Quixote*, and more like Lord Byron's *Don Juan*, and perhaps close to Captain Ahab's obsession over the great white whale, minus the whale. Aboard my own personal Pequod, I will encounter all kinds, all cultures, all of the exotic islands away from time, the delicacies of many women, fine foods, and along the way, I will discover the pratfalls. Apart from the journey, no one should look for a moral. Still, there is the problem of the central character, hermetically sealed, noetically enclosed, who remains a mystery, and the greater problem of a story with too many characters, all quickly moving across the stage and vanishing into the wings. The theologian, Martin Buber, would say I have an I/thou problem. I have no fully realized ego because I have not successfully reached out to you, I mean "thou"—and the thou that inherently exists in the me part. Or to "them," the people who traipse across my stage and then are heard no more. "Lo," I have not passed through the valley of the shadow of anima—as Jung might say it.

Marlon L. Fick

~ 17 ~

Logic Ends Where Africa Begins
or
The Adventures of Marcel de Vigny

I saw your face before I saw you . . .

Those first days in Africa were unreal. Had I paid more attention to geometric analogies and Boolean logic, with its categories of overlapping circles, I might have made some use of it now to describe exactly where one perception ended and another began: human and animal sweat overlaps with the circle of air, the air with lingering smoke from cook fires, the snapping of dry limbs from the fire with the ululations of song and drum in intricate rhythms doubling back on themselves into the same circle, a smell of warm stale beer and little rivers of beer into urine trickling down a dirt hill behind a row of wooden shacks.

Before leaving the coast for the interior, I had a few days to spend at the beach. The palm trees like one-legged dancers leaned west over the white sand lapped by the waves, decomposing the shore. Days I was not otherwise occupied, one of the guys from the embassy, seeing me on the beach, often stopped to talk. His name was Steve—short blond hair, slight build, not unlike myself but for the tattoo of an anchor on his right forearm. He was

71.

good with conversations, or rather good with questions. He asked a lot of questions. Normal questions with an occasional weirdness thrown into the mix. When I asked him something, I usually got evasive answers. In the course of a few days, I had learned that Steve was 27, from a farm in Iowa, worked at the embassy, worked on the roof of the embassy, knew something about remote sensing, and, oddly, when I guess he began to trust me a little, that his job involved listening to Colonel Muammar Khadafy's conversations.

—How do you do that?
—Just point the receiver and listen.
—What are you listening to him for?
—Intel.
—Isn't Khadafy in Libya?
—Yup.
—My, what big ears you have.

Our conversations were interrupted by the deafening roar of French fighter jets landing and taking off on a strip a few hundred yards away.

—Say what?
—A war with Chad.
—What for?
—'Cause he's a bad guy.
—So . . . all these French jets and Israeli paratroopers, they have something to do with this, I'm guessing.
—They're fighting the Libyan army right now. We're not directly involved. Strictly tactical.
—Right. Just listening.

It would not be the last time I ever saw Steve, but several years would pass before our paths crossed. It was, however, our last conversation, just before I was mustered *en brousse*—removed to the jungle. "Removed"—this was a term used by the Jackson administration. The American Indians were "removed to the west," uprooted, dispersed, given cholera, and ultimately slaughtered.

I could not have been more confused: He was talking about softball.

—Some of the staff at the embassy wanted to get a softball game together. You in?

—Sure, yeah. I love it.

—What position you like?

—Short. Center. Whatever.

—If I were to ask you to kill someone, would you?

He stared at me as if he were serious.

—What? No. You're kidding me.

He laughed.

—You're right. I'm kidding you. No, seriously, there is just this thing you could do for me. It would really help me if you could do it. I'd really appreciate it, and I'll even pay you.

—All right. I'm listening. I won't kill anyone, though.

—No. No. I wouldn't ask you to do that. Really, I was kidding. No. This is serious. You're going to Djidji tomorrow . . .

—Yes.

—There's this bad guy not very far from there.

—Like Khadafy.

—Worse. He teaches young kids how to fire Kalashnikovs.

—Okay.

—This guy. He has a half brother in Lisala. That's up from Brazzaville.

—That's over the border.

—Yeah. Not a problem.

—So what do you want? Say it.

—I want you to go to Djidji. I want you to make friends with this woman.

He showed me a picture.

—You want me to meet this woman, and . . .

—Sometimes she goes to Lisala to see her father. His name is Ngugi Ntamby.

—And Ntamby is the bad guy.

—Not exactly.

—So he's a good guy.

—He has a half-brother. It's the brother who's the real bad guy.

—You guys are pretty sure of who's naughty and nice.

—Oh yeah.

—Okay, so. Who's the bad guy?

—His name is Kabila. He isn't even in the Congo. He's in Zaire, but he keeps in touch with Ntamby.

—So then you want me to go to Zaire, too?

—Just get to be friends with this girl. When she goes to Lisala, you go with her. That simple. In a few months, when you're on your R & R, we'll talk again.

—I make friends with the girl in the picture. Name?

—It's on the back. Memorize it.

—Okay, I make friends with her and convince her to let me tag along to Lisala. I get into Lisala how?

Steve handed me a passport with a folded document inside. It said, "ATTESTATION D'AFFECTATION," the two things I needed to cross from Gabon into Zaire, and if need be, the Communist Congo. I stared at it. It had my picture. My name was "Marcel de Vigny," from Geneva, Switzerland. According to the document, I worked for the Red Cross. Like everything else in Africa, it wasn't real. It was unreal.

—I understand your French is pretty good, *sans accent*?

—It's okay.

—You shouldn't have any problems.

—So then, in Djidji, am I Marcel de Vigny? Or am I me?

—You're you. Only use that to get across the border.

—What if they ask this girl about me.

—Make sure they don't ask her.

—Whoa, man. This is dangerous.

—Not too. The Red Cross moves in and out of there all the time.

—I don't know . . .

—And this is a lot of money.

He showed me a check for five thousand dollars. I thought, *it isn't real* . . .

—Do this and it's yours.

I looked at the check. I looked at the picture of the girl. I looked at the fake paper and passport. I looked at the check again.

—This can't be real.

—Oh yeah. It's real.

—Ok, there's a thing I want to know.

—Anything.

—Is your name really Steve?

~ 18 ~

The Congo as Noetically Enclosed

Marie Ella and I are spending the weekend at the beach. It's good to be out of the jungle for a while. I am sitting on a fallen okoume tree on a beach this afternoon reading *Portnoy's Complaint* under some palm trees that lean at sharp angles west over the Atlantic Ocean. It's an overcast July day and Marie Ella has gone shopping in Old Akebe. I get no more than a few pages and can't remember what I've just read. But I remember remembering: tall, undernourished Marie Ella turning, walking slowly, gracefully in that ancient African way, slow and as graceful as a black, elegant wasp trailing its long legs through the air, as if to say *my people have been here for thousands of years, what we have known we have known for thousands of years, and this has taught us not to be in a hurry.*

I thought about how beautiful she looked sleeping. Her skin is so dark that she disappears on a moonless summer night more quickly than my whiteness, but in the tiny burst of a match to light the kerosene, her limbs shine like Japanese lacquer. . . . *mon petit chou, porquoi tu ne peux pas dormer, viens tu mes bras* . . . the pink underside of her hands, pink of her inner lips, such a whiteness in her teeth. She wore a small gold cross around her neck. At night, she took off her large man-framed, thick glasses and her eyes suddenly shrunk back to a normal proportion.

The drums and ululations began around dusk somewhere past the beaches reserved for the half-naked French women. When Marie Ella returned from Old Akebe, she brought tortoise ova, built a fire beside a beached okoume log, wrapped the ova in tinfoil, and buried them in the coals to broil. As the fire licked its way further into the side of the tree, we took off our clothes and went swimming. The water here is body temperature, womb temperature, and we wrapped our legs and arms together like a couple of male and female twins. I did not want to leave the water, ever. I remember knowing *the world has not heard from me for so long, the world has forgotten me* as if it had ever known me or ever would.

As Ionesco would say, *Comme c'est curieux, comme c'est bizarre.* How curious, how bizarre. The world in fact had not forgotten me. They had heard of me, or were about to hear of me. I wasn't around much, so I do not recall precisely when this happened. I was, in fact, "a commodity," or about to become one, but didn't yet know it.

The priest and philosopher of St. Louis University, Father Walter Ong, who mentored me in early youth, referred to the text as noetically enclosed and autonomous—as much so, I suppose, as any human being, by virtue (or by vice) of their subjectivity. Father Ong would not have approved of my life, but as I was his only non-Catholic pupil, he was under no special obligation from the Vatican to forgive me or hear my confessions: I—if "I" is or isn't a text—am noetically enclosed, a mystery to myself. I am hermetically sealed. Africa is also sealed.

Eventually I got out of the water. As usual my footprints disappeared behind me in the waves. I was taken, seized from Africa by invisible claws and quickly condemned to spending much of my life longing to return. After several months of dysentery and malaria, a pontoon plane landed on the Ogoué, down river from my village where the river was wide enough for the landing. The elder and his oldest son paddled me down to the plane. In my delirium, sweat, bloody shorts, I mediated a heated argument between a group of rabbits and porcupines. The rabbits argued that they were more delicious in peanut sauce and red pepper than the porcupines, and the porcupines were about ready to throw their quills when I assured them both: they were both equally delicious, and arguing that it was precisely because our lives are so short that they should stop to consider how best to lead these lives, as all of us would soon be simmering in a cooking pot, like me. I'm simmering in a cooking pot and brokering a peace between the animals and still I don't know it's malaria and bloody dysentery. The next solid thing I knew, from the shared world of common reference, was of being in a hospital in Paris.

—*Tout suite tu irais aux Etats Unis.* [Said a nurse, brusquely; not slowly, like a gracious African beauty, and not without grace, simply not African.]

—Où est Marie Ella?

She didn't answer me. I asked the doctor in English,

—Doctor, where in the hell is Marie Ella?
—I'm sorry, I don't know. You are in Paris. Paris, France. [He said, as if I were another stupid American who didn't know where Paris was—like Jesse's girlfriend who thought London was a country.]

—Why didn't you leave me there? I would have been fine.
—Monsieur, you weigh 38 kilos and you have lost a great deal of blood. Parasites ate through the wall of your stomach. You are stable now, so just rest, and when you are feeling a little better, perhaps you can enjoy Paris awhile before your government sends you home.
—I don't want to go home. I want Marie Ella. We're going to have a baby!

The doctor paused and looked at me. He took a brief moment to appear human.

—Maybe you will find some word from her among your things.

I think I passed out again. I don't really know.

~ 19 ~

The French Connection

I woke up and fell back to sleep. I dreamed the nurse was talking to me and woke up to the empty white room. I dreamed or I didn't. It was the doctor again, or it wasn't. A man was speaking in English, low, under the surface of consciousness. English.

—Are you awake, then?
—Where am I?
—Paris.
—You're not a doctor . . .

Then I see the doctor and the nurse. I dream they are standing, kissing at the foot of my bed in front of me. She's wearing nothing.

—No. I'm not the doctor. I'm Steve's friend.
—Steve.
—You remember Steve.
—Steve.
—Lisala? Remember Lisala?
—Um.

The doctor is naked too. White chickens are milling around on the ceiling, pecking at the ceiling upside down.

—You met Ntamby.
—Ntamby. Yeah. I know Ntamby.
—Then maybe you know things about Kabila.
—Ntamby's uncle. Why are they fucking in front of us?
—How popular is Kabila in Lisala?
—Oh everyone likes Kabila.
—I see.
—Why are they . . . right in front of us . . .
—No one else is here. Just me and you. I want you to remember Lisala.
—Who are you?
—I'm Steve's friend.
—Steve . . .
—How strong is Kabila in Lisala?
—Oh he is very strong.

I think I was singing . . .

—*He is strong, so very very strong and we are weak, but yes, Jesus loves me . . . yes, Jesus loves me . . . yes, Jesus loves me . . . the Bible tells me so . . .*
—How well armed?
—Two.
—What?
—He has two arms.

The doctor and nurse were about to climax. My fever she said is breaking. It's breaking! Oh! It's so cold. Oh! So hot! I am hot and sour soup. White room where the chickens are hot and cold and upside down, and dropping eggs on me.

~ 20 ~

The Desert

. . . Ezekiel's vision of dry bones . . . salted away . . . promiscuous tongues. . .

There was a crumpled and water damaged letter in my duffle bag. It was green and black on the outside from mold. It was in Marie Ella's perfect script in the best Sorbonne French . . . *Mon cheri, . . . I have gone to stay with my mother in Rwanda. I will write to you when I arrive to the address in Washington D.C. that I found among your things. Here is the address . . .*
Please come as soon as you are well.

What address in D.C.? Then it occurred to me, she must have found a business card from a hotel in D.C. where I had spent one night, over a year earlier, just before mustering out.

I went to the hotel in D.C. No letter there. Then flew to Arizona. I had spent a few days wandering aimlessly, dressed in African clothes, around Paris, mostly the Left Bank. It was chilly and I had nothing warm to wear, but I wanted to see my favorite places. I sat in the Cathedral of Notre Dame and shivered. The great mandala, the Rose Window, grew increasingly incandescent. *Oui, tu as raison, il faut apprendre à vivre avec les temps, le destin et si le Bon Dieu, veut vraiment que nous soyons ensemble, nous le serons, si nous continuons à être près l'un de l'autre.* Marie Ella was speaking to me. She believed in God and Destiny and Two Souls becoming One. . . . *que tu m'aimes autant que moi, que tu respires comme moi avec toi, que le moment jamais fini, que existe toi et moi . . .* She was never sentimental, except, it seems, in a quickly written letter stuffed in my duffle bag where it grew a black and green mold.

I walked out of the airport in Phoenix, dazed by the sun and a heat so different from what I had become accustomed to in Africa. There was a Mercedes, a BMW, a Rolls Royce, a white limousine, people in shorts and sandals and untucked shirts over their haughty paunches. The protruding rib cage and belly pooch of a malnourished child in the village of Djidji stuck in my mind as a taxi ushered me down an avenue in Scottsdale, past the McCormick Ranch. I apologized to the driver for being sick in his taxi. The next day I wandered the aisles of a supermarket, amazed by all the food.

I curled up and went to sleep. After sleeping for two days, I spoke for a while with my mother, briefly, and took the keys to one of the cars, and drove out to the desert hoping to find absolutely nothing. It is here, in the negative dialectic, that *not yet* collapses in *no longer* and *the nothing* gives birth to a vast horizon of *becoming*. I had a wife with child in Africa. We were a trinity of sorts, a unity of being across an impossible distance—given that I was penniless and unemployed. I stayed in the desert until conscious that I needed water. I drank a glass of water, knowing the water was already purified, free of disease, of cholera, schisto . . . And I went back to sleep for three days.

My college friend, Yarnie, was the only person I knew in Arizona. Yarnie and I met back in college on the steps of old Green Hall, the Athenian law school. He was sunning himself when we met and recognized that we had a class together in American literature. I suppose a few weeks went by before I realized that he was missing the first finger on his right hand and that he was older than I was by around ten years. When I got around to counting his fingers, he caught me counting and smiled, held up his hand and smiled a big gap-toothed smile and said,

—Yeah, the million dollar wound. Tet Offensive. One of the first medevac'd out of there. I was lying on my sandbags one minute—you know?—smoking a joint, and the next thing you know there's mortar fire all over the place. Pieces of shrapnel with little Chinese characters on them. I just tried to return fire, reached for a round and the fucking beehive went off with this hand over the muzzle. A captain said I did it to myself but I didn't, I mean it just all happened really fast. But it was great. One minute I'm smoking a joint and listening to Marvin Gaye, and the next, I'm walking wounded in Japan. Saw Kyoto . . . Nara . . . I couldn't have been any luckier.

After that, he openly shared his war stories, trying again and again to tell me what it was like. I watched Coppola's *Apocalypse Now* with him a half a dozen times, and every time he kept repeating,

—It's a metaphor, but that's how it was. Coppola is getting it down in Conrad's *Heart of Darkness* line: 'The horror. The horror.'

After a few days in bed, I called Yarnie and said,

—I've just come home from the Congo . . . you know . . . *the horror . . .*
—Say no more. I know a stripper who is gonna love you.

He even knew her name, "Candy," and her telephone number. By three in the morning, it was pretty clear that Yarnie was ready to go home. He wrote down Candy's number on a napkin and gave it too me, saying,

—No good for me. You know, Agent Orange pickled my dick a long time ago. You know [he said], if you sit very still in the desert, you can begin to see the tarantulas migrate by the thousands.

> There's a thinness in the bamboo hills,
> children hanging from dark nipples, three o'clock in the morning . . .

Two okoume trees have beached here side by side
and so we build a fire between them,

broil tortoise ova in the sand

then crouch and eat
as the fire licks into their sides
and the ocean dances the dance that turns into birth . . .

It is better to go out into the desert among the scorpions and tarantulas then spend another minute more among the rich and ludicrous because at least the scorpions and tarantulas show themselves as such. I was too ill to know this and Yarnie was an expert at putting a thing out of mind. Using his methods, weeks could pass without a single thought of Marie Ella. He must have done these things when he was on R & R in Saigon. Whores, strippers, drugs, alcohol—all miracles of pain relief. Morphine. A woman. Yarnie was momentarily passed out. After he came too, at six foot five inches, he was plenty strong enough to carry me out of Loose Lips on the outskirts of Phoenix and into the stars and the cold mesquite sweetened air. I still only weighed around 85 or 90 pounds.

—What time is it?
—Don't know. Almost morning.
—What year is it?
—1984, little brother.
—Thanks, big brother.

~ 21 ~

Heidegger and the Fall

On a Sunday, I alternated between watching the swans in Central Park and reading the newspaper. *Je ne sais pas exactement quel est le motif de ta dépression. J'aimerais autant être dans ta peau pour vraiment sentir comme toi et te comprendre.*

Do we dance tonight?
Do we sing? In the profane cave of the Colonel's mouth?

Woodsmoke rises.
The canopy is torn.
Crickets scrape their legs like a pair of fire sticks.

Vines root in the mind
and the river turns in the moon like a black snake bellied up...

This is how we find each other in the dark, as easy as
finding a wound,

we rub our legs and languish...
do you hear the tom-toms and the song?

Do you hear the Colonel coming?
His ribs have made our wattled walls.
His cane has touched us all.

So our clothes stay loose.
The night is dissolute.

Wet and lovely our mouths.
The night is wet and lovely.

At these intervals I remembered Yarnie and imagined his R & R life in Saigon with his exotic Vietnamese companion and wondered if he had children on the other side of the world, and wondered if he wondered. Oddly, our lives had already crossed at two times and two places—Kansas and Arizona. We'd meet again, years later, but by then we would both be past wondering. I was about to meet the vampire who was going to change whatever hope I had of life to an eternal longing for death.

A year went by in New York with hardly a care. I was at the top of my game academically, socially. I studied, worked as a copy editor for a press in midtown, went to parties, met the world's best artists, musicians, scholars.... I was soaring before the fall, the fallen-ness, whatever its name, the descent into hell or somewhere where neither beer nor books, nor even a fine woman could rescue me. At the core of Heideggerian thought is a feeling, in the word *sorge,* or the sorrow of fallen-ness, primordial sorrow, primordial care... whether it be crouching by the campfires at the beginning of time, or surrounded by the four little walls of an apartment in New York. In the abyss, all of us care for someone, or feel sorrow. This is sole in determining we are human, and, therefore, incapable of recognizing the face of evil when evil smiles, a dark night in winter in New York. Now I remember Yarnie saying about the film, *Apocalypse Now,* Francis Ford Coppola gets it, only he's doing it with a metaphor. Like that, I don't actually mean that Kay Sansouci, Kay Happy-Go-Lucky, was without primordial care or sorrow, just that I get it. It was a dark night in New York that gives the film noir first line, "It was a cold dark night in New York City…" an entirely new twist. It was Friday night. I was drunk. She was a little blurry, pale, pimply, pear shaped intellectual from the deep south. She was also a lesbian who knew less about sex with a man than a barnyard chicken—a metaphor, which, I learned from a Kansas farm boy is not always a metaphor. It was a matter of getting it over with and done.

But "over" was just the beginning. The very moment the dark angel conceived, she began to scheme like a Black Widow. What is the best way to beat a man down, make him think he rose from the very dust where we walk? I didn't even stay the night. She said something like, *oh, so that's all it is* and feigned a thank you but she didn't think she'd be doing such things again. Okay, fine, I was relieved. I even gave her a fake phone number, and I quickly forgot her. It wasn't the only time I'd ever gone away from "making love" feeling dirty, but it was far worse than Easter Sunday morning with Micki. Yet New York was a perfect place to put things behind you. The city changes from minute to minute and you change with it to stay in its groove. The other night the New England Life Building was illuminated in red, tonight it was violet. I staggered out of Eddie's only a few hours after the Vampire bit me and walked down Waverly Place to Washington Square. The WTC soared up into the damp winter mist and disappeared. I had wanted to be somewhere noisy and Eddie's was good for that, but after awhile a group of witless, pretentious wannabe poets began to annoy me and I opted for the noise in my own head in the 3 AM quiet of Washington Square. I wrapped a scarf around my neck, but I was too numb to feel the cold.

It was snowing in New York. Whatever noise there was of streets in nervous crisis fell under a blanket of snow that muffled and stifled even the smallest complaint. It was utterly unrealistic and sick with irony. I had not exactly sworn off women, it's just that I seldom had the urge to "date." The

African girls bathed in the Ogoué naked. Their mothers walked through the village baring their breasts. I looked down at a photo of Marie Ella. Children ran in and out of my mud wattle hut laughing and screaming. I looked at the picture of her in her African sari and couldn't make anything make sense. She was "out there," *being-out-there/Dasein.*

I have always had trouble with the Heideggerian reversal, making the outside into the inside, like Longfellow's Indian making a glove from the skin of an animal, making the fur side warm side inside into the cold side outside—which all sounds vaguely like surgery a transsexual must undergo. As for me, my cold side was inside. My warm side was outside.

I went back to my studies. I classified the past as a distraction. Women are a distraction. Friendship is a distraction. The allowable exception became a few conversations that might lead to a new insight, a new idea. Columbia was buzzing with semiotics, so I entertained semioticians and read their books. Michael Riffaterre spared me his books and explained his ideas to me in person. So did Umberto Eco, though later I caved and read their books. Just outside New York, at Yale, Harold Bloom was the champ of Derridean deconstruction, which I loathed out of my loyalty to Heidegger. How dare he take a perfectly articulated concept, already existent in Heidegger, and steal it. Deconstruction was already implicit in Heidegger's *"destruction"* in *"poesis"* –how dare this Derrida steal from Heidegger without so much as a footnote? I have vowed to give the most insignificant tryst a footnote. The vampire is a footnote, for Christ's sake. If she crawls back out of her grave on the next full moon, she is still a footnote. A cheerleader from high school with a fetish for handcuffs because her dad is a cop is still a respectful footnote— duly noted here. At least they're credited! Heidegger offered a way out of the abyss, the existential abyss. He began with sensitive critiques of the works of Nietzsche and vowed that he could find a way out of the abyss. He never gave up on faith and the faithful never gave up on him. When I met his student, Gadamer, who authored *Wahrheit und Methode*, I became even more convinced that language was not my enemy, as "arbitrary and slippery" as the new theorists assumed. If anything, their slippery signs had saved me more times than I'd ever known. This is a visceral awareness beyond their French cerebral tail chasing. I confess that I began the rumor that all French theorists are born with a tail—evolutionary throwbacks. The vast *oeuvre* of the deconstruction library boils down to our response to inescapable doubt and ambiguity, a problem I grasped and accepted years earlier, a Sunday morning when I gazed at that empty cross, wondering if it was the cross before or after. Was I yet to be crucified and condemned? By and by the vampire footnote may shed light on this problem.

I do, however, credit the deconstructionists for slowing down my life, making me think twice about my intentions. I toyed with the idea that intentionality sprang out of the idea of "the cult of personality"—hence there'd be an arbiter for meaning. Be that as it may, they made me more aware of how my words and actions might be twisted and raveled into rags.

My test results were positive. I had in fact been bitten by the vampire. Congratulations! you may say, and then hold up a mirror because I would not be there! Infected! Condemned! Or you might even try to picture me in those dead vampiric eyes of Sansouci, glassy and black and giving back nothing. Ms. Kay Sansouci (Ms. I-Could-Care-Less, Ms. I-Don't-Give-a-Shit) and her partner—who unbeknownst to me had been there with her, lurking in a shadow—had what they wanted, an unwilling donor because willing donors cost money.

In retrospect I don't blame them. They lived in a society that didn't recognize them, a society where, if you happen to be gay, you better be invisible. In such a place, where intolerance contaminates the air we breathe and the thoughts we think, those who are forced to live underground in eternal darkness must find ways to exist through subversion. In the case of Sansouci, society managed to twist her into a subterranean devil. They could never reap the rights and benefits of a traditional couple, couldn't claim two exemptions on their taxes, maybe didn't feel free to display their affection in public, and suffered in ways that I will never understand.

Were society fair and open, we could all have congratulated them on their grand fortune. But we didn't and don't live in an open society. I didn't even know the gender of their kid until two years later, a girl. Pass out the Cuban Cohibas. The Romeos and Julietas. The Julietas and the Julietas. I had a daughter. Whereas, I still didn't know anything about my child in Africa, what gender, and worse, where? Somewhere in Rwanda or Zaire, or the Congo? But characteristic of the great United States, who gives a good goddamn what happens in Africa? I had a child, a child of something like love or mutual need, born by both of us through nature and mutual intent, but where? I wanted a family too, but by now there was a civil war in Zaire and I was not sure if I'd ever see Marie Ella again. Maybe I will be permitted to look at the Sansouci kid's dental records if I pressed the court. I still had my feelers out, letters to the African and U.S. consulates on both continents, letters to Zaire, Gabon, Rwanda. The letters had all come back, crumpled, dog-eared, and unapologetically unopened.

~ 22 ~

Voyages 1

New York was a booster station, a refueling stop, a fresh launching pad into a life sinking deeper into debauchery, like the jumper who leaps without wings. I had a good education. I learned that writers have more fun—they have sex, drink, bed down whenever and whomever, and live in a perpetual state of Shelleyan sexual democracy. It wasn't for me anymore. I finished with school forever; the next day, I was on a freighter bound for Normandy where I had planned to catch a second freighter to West Africa. On the passage across the Atlantic, I only had one book, Carl Jung's *Modern Man in Search of a Soul*. Though reading on a ship that pitched forward and side to side on the Atlantic made me green, I persisted.

Jung was surely right to throw out the canonical approaches to logic. Every attempt I had tried to make by category failed. I could try to categorize my experience that way: Women who hate sex, women who love sex, and women who have not yet had sex, women who were simply people—all of these as aspects of my personal albeit fragmented self in the collective, rather than the grand collective unconscious. It was comforting to find that Jung seemed to accept some of Freud's basic premises regarding sexual repression as a cause of neurosis. I had seen this in women, of course, but it was years before I understood that men were not immune, especially just having been bitten by a vampire and utterly unable to find myself in the mirror, harder still to find myself again in a strange woman's eyes. The harder question is of course whether one can lose his soul in the very search for it. Nonrational science, or "the mystical"—I wasn't ready for Jung, certainly not surrounded by hundreds or thousands of miles of water.

A Greek freighter, with a few rooms for passengers, left New York Harbor in the middle of May and set a course for Liverpool, then Normandy. At either port I would have to find another ship bound for Africa, hopefully as close to Marie Ella as Port-Gentil, and I could go overland from there. My cabin was no bigger than one of those YMCA rooms in Chelsea, but I had a portal about 10 feet over the water line. Topside thre was a tiny area reserved for non-crew passengers. I was the only passenger. Before leaving, I wrote to my sister, sent her my stuff, and gave her power of attorney and access to my trust fund, which would last a couple of years, but it would buy me some time.

The English coast came cautiously into view, like Husserlian epistemology, first only a vague idea of the coast, then a shade of difference on the horizon, maybe mistaken for a band of low clouds, until finally, utter mathematical certainty of coast-ness. I was ready to be on land again instead of haunted awake or asleep by Carl Jung. The sea was not the sea one can explain with science. There lurks a moody and terrible god who in a moment changes from serene to tempestuous. I prefer science, though. I have enough ghosts already. But the sea taught me the origins of superstition in its utter lack of a good gestalt, a well-formed image. It exemplifies what the Germans call a *ganzfeld*, a vast nothingness that the imagination must rush to fill with contrivances, mermaids and monsters. Or worse, rumor.

The day the ship docked at Liverpool, I looked for ships out of Liverpool and Normandy. There were ships leaving for ports in the Middle East, The Americas, India, Northern Europe, the States, practically everywhere except for African ports. One ship was going to South Africa from Liverpool, but not for another three months, but even then, there would be another wall, Angola, which I would probably have to go around, and there was no easy overland passage North, from South Africa to Zaire or Rwanda. In fact, I would be geographically closer to Marie Ella in France than I would be in South Africa, so I opted for France, with the idea that I could cross through Spain and take a boat to Morocco and wing it from there down the western coast of Africa, even if I had to hitch-hike or buy a jeep.

After a week in England, I reached Normandy and looked for a way to Spain. There was a hostel in town not far from the border that was only around thirty-five francs a night, so I stayed there. Mornings I went for some bread and some coffee, and then came back to write.

Sometime about then I called my sister.

—It's late evening there, right?

—Bolivar, that you?

—Yes.

—Mom died.

—Oh?

—She died a couple of weeks ago. Her liver. She asked for you. She wanted to know if you would be here before she died.

—Anything else?

—You won some award. Something called "The National Book Award." I gave all those papers of yours to a friend who sent them somewhere for you.

—Where is father?

—Maybe at the house in Carmel. He might be in Las Vegas. He has someone new.

—Okay.

—Mom left you stuff, too.

—What stuff?

—Stuff. And a pile of bonds and some stocks. Split three ways.

—So I have some money then.

—Where are you?

—I'm on my way back to Africa.

The Nowhere Man

—Where in Africa?

—I'm not really sure. I'll call you when I know.

—Take care, little brother.

—Yeah, okay.

~ 23 ~

Unamuno Wept

I lightened my load of books I'd acquired in Paris, put the rest of my things in my backpack, paid the concierge, and spent the rest of the day walking to Spain. I put out my thumb for every car and truck. After a few hours, a small truck pulled over and a toothless, grimy old man leaned out of his window.

—*¿Oye, tío, a dónde vas?*
—*Voy al sur.*
—*¿Pero a dónde?*
—*Gibraltar.*
—*Pues ala.*
—*Gracias.*

In July it was good to be up in the mountains where the air was cool. The old man had a stop to make in San Sebastián, then we would be back on the road. He was glad to have company. I'm sure he had never met an American so to avoid a lot of questions I just said I was from France. One cannot tell otherwise from my accent, which is rather generic and difficult to place. The old man's name was Rafael, Rafa for short. He liked to tell me his civil war stories, proud to have fought for Francisco Franco on the side of all that is good and righteous. To hear him, you would think he saved

The Nowhere Man

Spain singlehandedly. He said he wept that day in 1975 when Franco died. We lost our father. The trains stopped running on time. Now you can buy pornography! I supposed it was better that I had kept quiet about my origins, or he may have associated me with the Lincoln Brigade, and I may have found myself without a ride again. When he finally learned that I intended to travel on to the middle of Africa, he huffed,

—*¡Esos negros!*

Whatever, I thought. *He's the driver.*

> *In the Port of Gabon*
> *the blind whip each other with their tails.*

> *In the Port of Gabon*
> *the Colonel dips his canker sore in a cup of tea.*

> *In the Port of Gabon*
> *the stones grow warm in the sun and fall asleep.*

> *In the Port of Gabon*
> *the sky turns to a fine palm wine*
> > *like a young woman's milk.*

> *It's a long way back from the verandah at the Dialog*
> *to Old Akebe Plain.*

> *One forgets many things along the way*
> *and a blind fish swims in your soul.*

I could see the old man was tired and I offered to drive. He was happy to take a nap. It was very hot now, somewhere in Andalucía. From behind the wheel, I saw the olive groves and the fields of yellow grass as far as I could see, and the soil turn from a yellowish red to a darker red. If my child were alive, my child would be about three years old. If . . . conditional. One does not assume any particular life expectancy of an African child.

~ 24 ~

Hegel's Forgotten Africa

I am walking and walking along the coast. There is a small light, very far. A blinking star. A lighthouse. I turn and see the blue waves of a riptide sweep what is left back into the sea . . .

The end of the road was Granada. From there, I took a bus to Seville. I did not stop to saunter around Granada like a tourist going to visit the Alhambra or visit the Gardens of Spain, nor did I hang around in Seville, not down by the river where students were dancing under the lights, nor did I watch flamenco dancers. I got on the next bus to Gibraltar. I had grown impatient, calm on the outside, but frantic on the inside. Marie Ella and the child may be the only decent thing in the world. A child from love—or as close as I was ever able to approximate "love." In Gibraltar I found a ferry to Tenerife that would connect with a flight to Brazzaville.

I had almost escaped the whole of Spain without a single philosophical thought, not even a Spanish philosophical thought, until the jet was taxiing down the runway. Then I remembered Unamuno: "There is sorrow that has no redemption. We should weep, not because it avails us anything. If we recognize the pervasiveness of hopelessness and despair, we can at least experience the brotherhood of man." There is a sorrow that has no redemption—that's just great. Add to that, we should weep. I had not been able to weep since childhood—when my sister went to college and when Charles killed my dog. I felt very angry, deeply angry.

A bell for seat belts woke me in time to look out the window at the aqua blue waters and white coral reef surrounding the island of Tenerife. Time islanded. People come here to get away from time because time turns eventually into death. It is a grand illusion, growing drunk by an exotic swimming pool with concrete waterfalls, that feeling of being immune from death—bikinis on bronzing beauties lazing in the sun on an island adrift in the Atlantic.

Why didn't Marie Ella simply go to the American Embassy? They could have easily tracked me down. But that is a stupid question. Marie Ella, like most of the world, detests "America." It only made matters much worse that she cared enough about Africa to join the Pan African Communist movement, a status that only escalated her hysterical fear and not unfounded paranoia of the American government. Code 214B of the State Department, in nonsensical circular obfuscating language, guaranteed that no Communists brave enough to register themselves as such would ever set foot on the holy and hallowed ground of the United States. Fucking Eisenhower and his idiotic cold war—a not-so-cold cold war, spreading its battlefields to the every part of the world. More died in battle during so-called detente than died in the First and Second World Wars, including victims of the Holocaust.

Code 214B . . . I have forestalled long enough any mention of Georg Friedrich Hegel, his *Philosophy of History*, as well as his *Phenomenology of Spirit*. He is, after all, important to a wider understanding of the "body politic," for it was Hegel who analogized the "State" as an extension of "Family," ideally speaking. He may be more current today than when he was revising the Greek dialectic to explain the spiritual progress of history. However, if our allegiance to the state is likened to our allegiance to the family, then, in contemporary terms (indeed in his own day), we're in big trouble. I barely knew "my family," and I sure as hell did not know to what "government" I belonged. Geopolitical boundaries are in constant disarray. This in turn, I would argue, has a more dastardly affect on "the family" than the analogy to the contrary. At the core of his thought, however, there is still the unquestionable progression of sorts in the marriage of thesis and anti-thesis, producing synthesis. Whether or not "the body" is "politic," it is certainly natural and biological: boy (thesis) meets girl (antithesis). They argue, disagree, make up, fuck. They have a baby (synthesis), and so on. However, I love the notion of "Fate" clashing with "Freedom," and then fusing into a single totality—your fate is your freedom. I argued this with Octavio Paz years later, after he had integrated these ideas into his *Labyrinth of Solitude*, to characterize the ironic, existential fissure that exists at the core of the Mexican heart due to the unwelcome infusion of Spanish and Indian blood, a conflicted state of being which he asserts is a universal condition that is simply more visible among Mexicans.

In the world of clearly defined "nationalities," Marie Ella was left out of Hegel's equation. The United States State Department code 214B, under Eisenhower, made sure to drive a wedge between any family, despite any cross-fertilization across political boundaries. The code permits U.S. Immigration officials to deny any foreign born person the right of entry into the United States, and it was designed specifically to keep potential communist spies off of U.S. soil. Of course, it has been even more broadly interpreted since the '50s to include just about anyone, even poor Mexicans who want a chance to pick lettuce for a dollar more a day.

The next airplane landed in Brazzaville. A soldier in jungle camouflage stuck the muzzle of his machine gun between two of my ribs while another flung my clothes out of my backpack. He held up one of my shirts as if he were shopping.

—*Si te veux . . . un petit cadeaux.* ["A gift," I said. "Take it."]

He turned into smiles and graciously thanked me. His partner raised his machine gun while I stuffed my clothes back in the pack. I stepped outside and noticed the heavy steam that passes for air and permeates everything, rusting everything, pylons and tin shacks, empty barrels, even the laterite mineral in the dirt, the color and taste of dry blood.

I found a shack where a woman made Cameroon food with good *piment* oil—just a few drops. It is the hottest food I have encountered anywhere in the world. I ordered rice, goat, peas and applied a trickle of *piment*. A rat watched me eat from a chewed hole in the corner of the shack. It was too late that day to look for a boat going up river, going up that far, to Lisala, where Marie Ella had a half brother, whom I'd met just once, so I found a tin bar and drank a few beers, shared cigarettes with strangers that came into the bar, and promised to be friends with all of them forever, this being a custom. I posed for a photograph with one fellow and promised that I would be his friend forever. When they asked me where I was from, I said,

—*Moi, je suis russe.* ["Me, I'm Russian."]

And everyone was happy. I managed to find a hotel and sleep, though it was already morning. Actually, I dared to use my old Swiss passport and Red Cross document at the airport, but it worked.

The next day, I went to the docks at the river and talked to some boys. I found one, about 13, who reminded me of a clever boy I knew in Djidji, so I offered him a hundred CFA, Central African French francs, to take me up river to Lisala. Plus his gas. It was a lot of money to him, and he took his job seriously. I drank warm beer and watched the big dopey birds swoop in and out of the clearing the Congo cuts through the rain forest, and the crocodiles, and the hippos spewing water and wallowing in the mud along the banks, and I fell asleep in the boat.

It rained all through the night.
I could not hear the others making love.
In the morning she brought me tea with quinine in the leaves, some rice
I am too sick to eat
so she just sat by me, part shadow
in my blindness and her negritude.
I could feel her youth, a spirit like gazelle,
        surviving infancy, she had good years yet left.

I don't remember any of that dream.
The air smelled strangely green, mud walls
faintly like a woman's sex. No windows, doors
        or privacy.

A circle burned around that place
where the boys used machetes to hold the jungle back.
Sun baked red clay to a hard resolve,
and nights
it didn't rain
there was the Southern Cross to keep the faith,
though that too was many light years from today.
And I still wander through that village like a ghost.

~ 25 ~

A Child Bride

Marie Ella's half-brother, Makebe, was ubiquitous. I only had to ask a few people where I could find him. I'd met him only once at Steve's request. But Makebe remembered me as if I had only been away for one day.

—How are you? How is Marie Ella? [He asked in French.]

They did not have the same mother. Their father had three wives, at least three when I was medevac'd out of neighboring Gabon.

—So you have come from Paris?
—No, New York. I'm looking for Marie Ella.
—You are not with Marie Ella and your baby in Paris?
—I have not seen Marie Ella since the day they took me.
—I thought you were with her in Paris. My father, before he died, said that her last letter to her mother said that you were all Parisians now.
—I am sorry to hear about your father.

Suddenly there was an uncomfortable silence. Makebe broke it.

—So, you need to know . . . where . . . in Paris that you can find her.

—Yes. I need to know. I am sorry.

—No, I am sorry. Because, I do not know. Marie Ella is from Mother No. 1, and I am from Mother No. 3. I do not know her address. Perhaps our uncle Kabila knows . . .

—Kabila?

—Well, perhaps he would know, but no one discusses where he is. It is for his safety.

—I believe that she went to her mother, Mother No. 1, to visit her in Rwanda.

—I only heard that she had gone to Paris to be with you and see that your daughter would be in the finest schools, and be educated, like you.

—A daughter . . . *Une fille* . . . . *Une fille* . . . [I repeated, in shock and happiness and dismay and frustration; I still did not know where to find her, or them.]

Makabe looked embarrassed for me.

—*C'est normal!* Look, it is so common. So natural, these things. Wait! Wait here!

Makebe went into the kitchen and came back with a bottle of Gordon's gin, which he poured into two Dixie cups, filling them to the top. I noticed his children who had been staring at me with moon size eyes. One of them, a little boy, yanked at the long hairs on my very white leg and giggled. Then they all giggled and took turns yanking on the very long hairs on my very white skin. Makebe gave me a Gabonaise bleu—a non-filtered cigarette that tastes and smells like burning creosote—and one of his wives came in with a kerosene lamp just as rain began to fall and spatter against the corrugated tin roof of his small house. We talked late into the night. Makebe got drunk much faster than I did and offered me his first born daughter, said I could take her back to Paris with me and she could be my second wife. Lying through the fumes of gin, I agreed to take her so that I wouldn't offend him and turn his drunkenness into a sudden rage.

—I must confess she has not had the bleeding that makes her a woman, but I think it will be anytime. If you are a patient man, you may take her with you. I know you are an honorable man and you will wait until she bleeds until you marry her. Until then she will be your sister and you will only pay me 500 francs because we are family.

—*Bien sûr, Makebe. C'est un honneur.*

I looked at the 10- or 11-year-old child and smiled at her with no intention of accepting his offer. It was amazing—they know, at that age, when they are being auctioned off, and for exactly what price. I turned my eyes away from her and resolved to leave as soon as I had drunk him under the table, proving that at least on some occasions it is most beneficial to be a hardened and hearty drinker, strong enough to defeat your opponent by not being the first to pass out.

~ 26 ~

Huck's Prophecy

My faithful little pilot Huck was asleep in the boat when I woke him and told him to get underway. The rain was brief and now we had a moon to see by. I told him to go back to sleep and I took the rudder. In the morning he took it, and I went to sleep. By the afternoon of the next day, I was back in Brazzaville. I did not know Marie Ella's last name. Even the son of Mother No. 3 did not remember the woman's name. I could not get a plane to Rwanda if I had known where to look in Rwanda, nor could I look in Paris without an address. There were a lot of women named Marie Ella and I did not have a photograph. I could barely picture her, the face of a thin woman, with man glasses.

I paid the boy for his work and he stared at the money in disbelief. I patted him and told him thank you three or four times, and then I walked around the streets of Brazzaville looking at the food piled on mats woven from dry grass, the monkeys cooking in big pots, spits turning young goats stuffed full of couscous—visions of things I love. I felt both elated and sad. Then, there in the market, my little Huck suddenly appeared out of nowhere with something in his hand, something for me.

—Take this. [He said.] It will make you strong and help you find who you are looking for.

—It was a chicken claw with feathers tied to it, a fetish, and I chose to believe.

~ 27 ~

Voyages 2

I never made a single conscious decision that directed the course of my life. Decisions found me. As a wise and elderly Baptist church lady in St. Louis once observed,

—You are a person incapable of judgment—whether for good or for bad. You simply do not make judgments.

I didn't understand that at the time. In retrospect I do. If she had been born Mick Jagger, she might simply have said that I had painted everything black. There was only one ship leaving from Africa and it was an Argentinean ship bound for Cuba—with a large cargo of iron ore, plantain, and okoume wood for paper mills. The passenger quarters allowed for six. But very few people enjoy traveling this way anymore. So I looked forward to a long passage undisturbed, but the trip was interrupted by another passenger whose name was Myra.

Myra was from Buenos Aires where they speak Spanish but pretend they are speaking Italian, using the affected inflections of Italy to sound more like old Europeans. I could but barely make out myself in her un-dappled, very blue eyes—this Myra Rickamann from Buenos Aires.

I should title this chapter of my life *Fear and Loathing on the High Seas*. This ship pitched and lurched, riding the swells of the ocean. Myra put me to use practicing her English.

—What write you? *¿Es tu diario?*
—*Sí, es mi diario.*
—*¿Escribes algo de mí?* Is *de* me?
—No.
—I want that you should to be know I really really sorry and how you say carry away. *Lo siento mi amor.*
—Well it would be rather nice to let it rest awhile.
—Rest. Ok. *Descansa. Tu pene, descansa.*

Her eyes were an alluring shade of blue. I have not been able to remember the names and faces of many people, and hence my difficulty in describing after so many years. As this is a true account, I have resisted the impulse to make up a face I can't recall. Of Myra I remember her blue eyes and that I asked her,

—Why are your eyes blue?
—Oh that is because my father is Nazi. No. Not now Nazi. He live at Buenos Aires with mine *muter . . . mitad Italiano y mitad indigenous.*
—What were you doing in Africa?
—*Algo . . . secreto por mein Vater.*
—What, smuggling diamonds? [I joked.]
—*Secreto.* Sometime I you tell.
—I'll tell you.
—No. I you tell.
—Okay.

~ 28 ~

Ideologies

When the Argentinean ship set anchor just off the waters of the Port of Havana, Myra did not go ashore, but she cried when we said goodbye, very embarrassing, and her German blue eyes filled with tears and redness as if somewhere in their pools a school of sharks were feeding on a seal. There I could see my reflection.

I went ashore with a few members of the crew. It is easier to enter Cuba from another Communist country than it is from the United States and the area then called "Congo," not neighboring Zaire, was a Communist nation supported by the Cubans. Also, I had my laminated party membership card from the days of Rodger.

Still I was questioned thoroughly. All this was in Spanish.

—How long have you been a member of the Communist Party?
—Since 1980.
—Are you still active in the Party?
—Yes, I just went to Africa to meet with a group of trade unionists.
—What do you want to do while you are in Cuba? Do you want to spy?
—I'm not a spy. I only want to visit your country.
—Who do you know in Cuba?
—I don't know anyone, but if you call your embassy in Nicaragua, I'm

sure they have their people in El Salvador and they can help you verify that I was a very close friend of Rodger Bland.

—We know of Comrade Bland. John Reed of the Americas.

—Well then you can probably find me somewhere in his writing.

—Would you like one?

It was a Romeo and Julieta cigar, not the Dominican Republican copy either. The actual Cuban.

—Yes, comrade, I would very much like one.

—Now then, what do you do?

—I'm a writer.

—What do you write about.

—Social responsibility and revolution, mostly.

—I see. I see. You will write about Cuba?

—If I write anything for Cuba, it will be for *La Gramma*, if they will have me. I assure you I will not attempt to publish anything without submitting it to the *Union de Escritores y Artistas* for approval.

—You're answers are very good, Comrade Collins. Now, tell me. Why "Bolivar."

—It was my father's idea of a joke, I think.

—I don't understand your father's joke.

—I don't get it either.

The Romeo and Julieta was so savory that I didn't mind the questions. I had the good sense to toss the Swiss passport and papers overboard before we reached port, and just enter, trying to hide nothing.

—Was your father a Communist?

—I don't know. I do not know him very well. I do know that he believed in spreading independence. [The next part I lied about:] And that he gave me a copy of *Das Kapital* for my 10th birthday and told me to read it.

—And did you?

—Did I what?

—Read *Das Kapital*.

—Of course.

—Do you wish political asylum in Cuba? Are you running?

—I'm not running. I'm just traveling for the time being.

—You have broken no laws?

—No.

—Tell me more about your relationship with Comrade Bland.

—We were best friends in college. We organized many protests against the United States. Rodger went to work for the Trade Unionists in El Salvador and he was killed there in the war.

—That, any CIA would know.

—Probably, but a CIA would not get a personal letter from his sister just weeks after his death.

—Do you have the letter?

—Not with me.

—You claim you were best friends to one of the most respected heroes of this century and yet you cannot produce proof. Comrade, I am not convinced that you are not a spy.

—Why won't you contact your people in El Salvador and Nicaragua and just do some checking.

—Comrade Bolivar, I am afraid we are going to have to. In the meantime, you will be detained.

I swear this on a stack of Baptist hymnals. The interrogation room was a concrete bunker with a single light, a table, and two chairs. To enter the room, we went through two doors, each requiring a different key. I thought the ghost of Stalin himself was going to be waiting on the other side.

The agent left the room and left me sitting there for over an hour. Then another agent entered and escorted me to a detention cell apologetically.

—It is . . . just until we can get this all sorted out.

My cell was isolated from other cells. It had a narrow bed with a moldy mattress and a bucket for drinking water and another bucket for use as a toilet, unemptied since the last occupant. No toilet paper. For dinner a guard brought me some rice and black beans. The small cockroach milling around in the rice like a child of the Khmer Rouge was complementary.

I was held for three days which I think now in retrospect was not very long considering the morass of bureaucracy in that country. My only visitor was a male nurse who came to draw blood and explained that it was mandatory for anyone entering the country from the Congo where SIDA/AIDS was infecting millions of people. If I had contracted AIDS, they would let me know. Otherwise, not to worry. No one ever contacted me.

Finally, with no apologies, the agent who had conducted the interview greeted me at my cell and walked me through a maze of halls and doors to the outside world. My pack was returned, minus half the cash I'd had in there, leaving about 700 U.S. dollars and 100 or so in Central African francs, and a few Spanish pesetas.

~ 29 ~

A Home Life

It was a little after noon, an oppressive day in September, and I spent the rest of the day walking around in Old Havana asking here and there about a room. The hotels were too expensive. I needed just a room somewhere. It struck me that the children did not come running along behind me asking me a bunch of questions, but I surmised that Havana still had tourism. By evening I had not found a room. Instead, I found Renee Chaurand, a tall, finely shaped woman of African decent and green eyes, loitering on the boulevard that runs along the harbor.

She was friendly and professional and eager to show me a room I could have. Oddly, the price of Renee and room was less than the European youth hostels. For 10 U.S. dollars I could have them both, every night. I only wanted the room and that was fine with her.

Renee's room was partitioned into two with a rope to suspend three blankets between her bed and a bed where her two little girls slept. Down the hall there was a common bathroom that I estimate around twenty-five people used. There were tall narrow Spanish colonial doors that opened onto a small terrace where she fried bananas, grilled a fish and made coffee.

I went right to sleep. I just kissed her on the cheek and told her I needed to sleep. I felt her leave to go back to the street, but she was back and sleeping soundly when I woke the next morning. I watched her, the beautiful stranger. I parted the hanging blankets and looked in on her little ones who seemed about the ages of three and five. The smaller one's arm lay across her lighter skinned sister's face. I left a note on a fruit crate beside Renee's sleeping head and went out.

Outside in the street, there were the first rustlings of early morning sounds, drunks stumbling in after the night, others waking up, someone starting an old truck, the squeak of rope and pulley stringing a cortege of condemned and empty shirts to hang over the alley. A cart wheeled up the cobblestones drawn by a horse and edged its way between a baby blue '57 Chevy and a chartreuse '49 coupe. I recognized the '49 from a Bogart movie starring a young Ida Lupino. It was their get-away car. Bogart played a bad guy with a good heart. She doesn't mean to but she gives him away, tells the authorities where they can find him providing they don't harm him. In the end he is surrounded. And the one who loves him the most, his dog, leaps from a police car and scurries up the mountain to greet him, letting the sniper take aim and fire the fatal shot. Dogs do not comprehend the concept of deception. Whether they are above or below the ability to do so, I do not know.

Time just came to a halt in Havana. Now and then, you might see a Yugoslavian car from the '70s, but for the most part, the importation of technology stopped at the time of JFK's embargo. I thought they were better for it.

That day I bought an airplane ticket and found a place in Renee's room to hide it. There were only a few places I could have flown: a few South American countries, and Canada and Mexico. Mexico was the cheapest. I wasn't in any hurry to go anywhere, just being realistic. My jailor had already shortened my stay in Havana by borrowing half of my cash and Cuban banks didn't receive wire transfers from the U.S., especially for someone posing as a deceased American author—though not officially declared as such. I didn't know I was dead until much later. I did not know the State Department was considering me "a spy"—though it was not clear to me for whom I was spying.

I also discovered that telephone calls weren't possible and mail was pretty iffy too. It was an island in every sense. You can't help but admire their tenacity, standing up to the big bad neighbor to the North and not just rolling over like the rest of Latin America. The little Star of David in the Caribbean did not even tremble as it stood in the shadow of Goliath. And his children went without milk and enough fruit. His farm cooperatives did not quite reach out to every mouth. The Soviet Union sent a little wheat and Spain tossed them a few pesetas. An island of ideology—it's a geographical metaphor and a reality that befits any predetermined set of rules for thinking. Perhaps true, Cubans were the most literate people on earth, but paradoxically they remained just as ignorant as anyone who lets an authority decide for them what they can and can't read. As I looked at all the books available, in the libraries and filling whole tables in the small city parks, I was rather surprised to see enormous gaping holes. Here: five separate accounts of the martyr, Che Guevara, killed by the CIA (pronounced *see ya*, as in *see ya later*) in Bolivia. Here: the complete works of Lenin and Lukács, two of Rodger's favorites. Here: a stack of Gorky's *Mother.* Maybe the books piled up for sale were for sale because they were so heavy and old and people had grown tired of the code—whatever the hell code it was—the way Americans had long since stopped paying attention to *The Constitution* and *The Bill of Rights.* In New York I'd once met an exiled Cuban poet, Maria Elena Cruz, who had spent 12 years in prison for publishing an unauthorized edition of her love poems, which I think are outstanding. They arrested her when she was 18, and she never saw life as it should be seen by someone in her twenties. In Cuba I met and later befriended a couple of writers who I thought were going to spit on the ground in disdain when I mentioned her name. They shook their heads. One of them said . . . . "decadence." The other one, "no one more lazy than that traitor." I tried to think of a writer I could say that about. It occurred to me—me! Or perhaps I could muster some negative feelings for Danielle Steele. I was consoled by the Americanism that I am free to not read her if I chose. Now it gives me pleasure to imagine—as long as such things remain only in the imagination—Steele being arrested, tortured, and executed for her crimes against humanity, or Art. Alas, she is miserably sick with wealth and discontent, bent everyday over her toxic martini. There is Karma in politics—I'm convinced.

Renee was frying bananas for the little girls when I came back the middle of morning. I could not find a grocery store, but I found some candy for the two little girls. There were neighborhood food distribution places, but the people who gathered to wait in line had vouchers. Renee told me where I could find the black market, so later I went there, bought a small bag of potatoes, some canned meats, and a liter of milk. Renee had run out of her allotment of milk vouchers. Kids under the age of seven are allowed to drink milk, but Renee said it was gone by the second week of the month.

She wanted to go dancing that evening and asked me to take her. I asked

—And the children? [I asked.]

It was a stupid question. Everyone in Cuba looks out for the children.

—They will be safe here. [She said.]

But in the following days, Renee let me take them to the park. I usually picked up a used book and set them to work on a project, like building a grand palace in the sand box, while I read. Noelia was five and Sophia was three. These outings let Renee catch up on her sleep.

We drank a few mojitos and danced. She perspired easily and soon she was shining under the white Christmas lights. The way she danced . . . as if she commanded every atom she possessed and directed their moves with the grace of a thousand starlings rising and twisting—each in concert with the rest, coming to rest on the outstretched limbs of a tree.

When I looked in her eyes, I couldn't see myself looking back. Then I kissed her because I liked her and respected her and I told her that. I told her I wanted her but that she did not have to agree. She could still be my landlord if she wanted to be, and she could just be my landlord. I would leave her alone and wouldn't ask again. But then she kissed me in a way that wasn't measured by a clock. She was comfortable. We became lovers and I soon forgot I had a plane ticket under the floorboard of that dilapidated apartment.

After a few months I had made a few friends and had somehow gained notoriety. A local newspaper ran an amusing article, too, about a "deceased" American author, age 25, who lived in Old Havana, married to Renee Chaurand, age 26, with their two children, Noelia and Sophia—the journalist was facetious about my being "deceased," quoting an American newspaper. Anyway, the article was more about Renee than me, given they didn't really know much more than I was a "missing writer" from the United States. Renee was a child of Cuba and *La Lucha*, the historic struggle against oppression. Her father and grandfather were killed by imperialist forces in the battle to save Angola from capitalist functionaries bent on world domination and worker exploitation—their bodies brought home and buried with honor. The article didn't mention her mother. So I let her tell me about that. Her mother remarried and lived in Havana, but she disapproved of Renee. Half the women of Cuba had to sell their bodies to feed their kids and her mother "disapproved." I disliked her instantly and Renee never brought it up again. I could see that it hurt her to tell me.

~ 30 ~

Marriage

Renee stayed away from other men. She wasn't the sort of person to proclaim her feelings, but she made it clear through subtle means that I was her only man. I bought the nicest ring I could afford and married her. On our wedding day we threw a party after the civil ceremony and everyone danced, even her mother. I was surprised to meet her mother. Renee was adamant that she would not be invited, and then she changed her mind, called her from a public phone—her stepfather owned a telephone—and both of them showed up for the party.

All night Renee hung on me, happy and a little drunk. When she wasn't hanging on me, Noelia hung on one of my legs and little Sophia hung on the other.

By this time I had managed to get word to my sister that I wasn't dead. "I'm dancing in Cuba. Tell them all to stop saying I'm dead. Also I am married." The Cuban government helped me send this short message to my sister by having the Mexican Embassy act as a go-between.

A neighbor loaned us his red and black 1959 Chevy Biscayne—which vaguely resembled the Batmobile, without the slotted seats and rocket tail—as a wedding present to help us with our honeymoon, so we drove to Santiago. Renee had to be back in three days because she had a new job as a tour guide in the Museum of the Revolution, and I had articles to turn in to the Union publishers. Cuba had granted me the right to work. I was even given a small grant to write a book. I say it was small, but it was more money than Renee could ever imagine and she nearly fainted when I showed her the check and letter from the Ministry.

Renee was born in Havana and had never been to Santiago or anywhere else. So we went on a site-seeing trip. First, we went to *Finca La Vigía*, the house where Hemingway lived just outside Havana on a hilltop. Then we drove to Santiago. She wore a beautiful white cotton dress on the last evening of our honeymoon and glanced down at her ring finger a lot as if she were afraid that God might suddenly take away her happiness with the stroke of lightning. She reminded me of Audrey Hepburn in her smile, though different in race. Like all Aristotelian categories and cubbyholes, they break down. Renee was both down-to-earth and ephemeral, other worldly, exotic, and real—something a philosopher can't grasp, though I was beginning to understand. It dawned on me it had been a long time since I looked for myself in her eyes. Rather, when I looked at her, I saw her.

~ 31 ~

An Invitation from Fidel

But if Renee was happy with how things had gone thus far, I don't think she could have been any prouder of me than when the President and Protector of Sovereignty cordially requested our presence for an informal dinner with him. She had Castro's letter in her fist and shook it hysterically, calling to all of our neighbors and the rest of Havana. She made sure that most of the island knew that she, Renee Chaurand de Collins, and her husband Bolivar Collins, were going to meet the President of Cuba. That night she surprised me again. She asked me,

—You are . . . a communist, aren't you?
—Yes, my love.

Her sudden trepidation turned instantly back into happy tears and she threw me on our bed, yelling to Noelia and Sophia to hurry up and play with the neighbor children and not come back for an hour.

I bought Renee the best dress I could find for the occasion. It was peach chiffon and had small fake golden beads and light pink rose petals hazily imprinted in its design. She was gorgeous and I am sorry Fidel if you are still alive to read this, but I wanted to ditch your dinner party then and there to be alone with my wife.

That was the middle of a January. By now I had learned to look at calendars to remember what weather was like up in the North. Three cars of state pulled up in front of our building and the neighbors started yelling at us to hurry.

The security officers smiled at us, and an official opened the back door of the second car, giving us a bow to indicate "get in." Renee whispered in my ear that she was about to pee with excitement and I said it would be best to wait.

President Castro divides his time among several locations partly out of fear of the dissidents, but mostly after many CIA attempts on his life. Must I remind anyone that his only best friend, if Che could be called "a friend," was tracked down and killed like a dog in Bolivia? Whatever judgment one thinks they must pass out of knee-jerk ideological allegiance, one cannot call him a coward, rather at the least, grant that Castro is a practical man. And given the world's tyrants, Castro was perhaps the least tyrannical member of that club.

He shook my hand and kissed Renee, though not with any gusto, yet it was a moment Renee would later turn into a story and tell for the rest of her life until she was sure that all of Havana knew it, and half of Santiago.

—So, you are a writer and I like writers, so I have asked you to visit me. I hope this does not inconvenience you.

It was fairly obvious from his demeanor that he did not really care if he inconvenienced anyone.

—Not at all, Your Excellency.

Just being there paralyzed Renee. She looked like a deer with her eyes stuck in headlights.

—Renee? What will you have to drink? Bolivar?

—Renee likes mojitos. I'll drink beer.

Castro motioned to his servant to bring the drinks.

I asked for a beer because I was not about to get drunk in front of one of the greatest political figures of the century. I needed to stay very sharp and something told me that I was standing on a precipice, dangerously close to falling. "Relax" and have an enjoyable evening with Fidel. He spoke to Renee a little gruffly, as if a brute of a man were trying to imitate a gentleman. He was awkward in small gatherings. Perhaps he was best at home, "socially," managing all of society, pulling its strings—in this way he would never have to be bothered with interpersonal details.

—Renee! [He said.]

She was hard not to notice, no matter how old one's age or how high one's position.

—Renee! Do you know how famous this man has become in his country?

—No . . . No sir.

—Well, first they all thought he was dead. Lost in Africa.

He didn't laugh. In fact, he never laughed at anything. He had said this matter-of-factly. If anything his tone was flat, disinterested.

—*The New York Times* said he had last been seen in Spain, San Sebastián, Spain, but reporters learned from his sister that he was traveling to Africa, where they assume everyone dies.

Castro paused, maybe realizing too late that his words could upset her. He had to have been briefed on how her father and grandfather died in Angola, but other people's feelings were clearly none of his concern.

—Then he arrives in Cuba because there is only one ship from Brazzaville.

I knew Renee had never heard of Brazzaville and we had never spoken of the past. I began to fear that the President might tell Renee more than I had had a chance to tell her.

—It seems they have it right now. *The Times of New York* has printed a more accurate account. That he is here with us. And we are pleased to have him, no? He can be of some use to us, perhaps.
—Yes, sir. [Renee said.]

Turning to me, Fidel Castro asked,

—How do you account for yourself?

I addressed him as Fidel to gauge his response, but he didn't smile. There had been a time when he did, but that was years ago. Now he seemed to struggle with idle talk and any talk at all came out edged with sarcasm and sprinkled with vulgarities that coated the general malaise of bitterness. Truly, he was a match for Richard Nixon.

—Fidel, I really don't know. I spoke to my sister by telephone, which I have not been able to do since I was in France and I only learned from her about the book.
—So you came to Cuba because you want to be like Hemingway.

Castro respected literature, much more so than the other arts, but his comment was caustic rather than complimentary.

—Hardly. As you said, it was the only boat, but I am very happy to be here. I have come to love your country deeply. And you, sir, are someone for whom I have a respect beyond my abilities to express.

—*No me jodas.* ["Don't fuck with me."]

He pulled a book off a shelf. It was my book. The last time I saw it, it was a stack of loose papers tied together with ribbons and tossed into a box addressed to my sister.

—Such an odd topic, this missionary translator taking the printing press to Kansas, subduing the Indians with the opiates of religion and then fucking them . . . it struck me as honest. I agree with your American reviews. You alone have told the story of your country's holocaust. Every ghastly detail and the imperialist-what-is-his-name . . .

I had not set out to write a political book, but Castro read it politically as he did with every work of literature. This reminded me of Rodger.

Renee looked at me with a puzzled face. She did not understand "holocaust," "missionary," or "Kansas." She knew the words "Spain, France, Africa," but she seemed distressed at the prospect that there was more to me than being her husband and lover, adored by Noelia and Sophia. I felt her anxiety.

—Oh... What was his name? [Castro said again.]

—Andrew Jackson. He initiated much of the genocidal practices and the strategies to remove to the west, to Kansas in 1829, various tribes that he knew could not coexist and would simply die from killing and disease. Really, it did not take a genius. They behaved then much like Africa's warlords today.

—And now your students, in all of the academies, are learning the truth. And like me they are eager to seek out the source of this news, which is you, Mr. Bolivar Collins, in Cuba.

—That's news to me.

—No. It is true. Not only are your students required to confront their own history of imperialism and destruction, but you have started a movement . . . for the social good. Despite all the Ronald Reagans. But we will outlive them too. We will bury them, like Khrushchev promised.

—I hope so too. [I lied.]

He cut a Cohiba and handed it to me. Renee was lost in the conversation and sipped on her mojito. While Renee was trying desperately to put out the terrible fires of misshapen gestalts forming in her brain, mine were coming into view with clarity. I had written the novel in college.

Dinner was announced and we sat at the table with the President for chicken, vegetables, and rice—which I only remember because Renee repeated it so many times to me and the neighborhood until all of Cuba knew what we had for dinner.

—Honestly, Mr. President, I wasn't totally aware of an ideological agenda when I wrote the story. My friend, Mr. Rodger Bland . . .

—Yes, I know of Mr. Bland! A comrade like you!

Renee beamed with pride at those words.

—Killed by the greedy pigs who learned to kill like that in Georgia—at "school!" [He humphed.]

—The Sioux were pretty savage too. In fact they had pretty much purged most of the Konza, the Kansas Indians, before the first white outpost in the west. The remainders died of cholera and yellow fever. I wouldn't exactly call that a class war either.

Renee could not follow the conversation, but she understood what wars do, and she shrunk from a vision of how I might be taken from her and named "a martyr." She shrunk with a quiet fear, while I, one the other hand, had eaten enough chicken and drunk enough beer to interrupt the President...

—Here's the thing. *Pasa así.* A left wing in my country does not mean we long for tyranny, Mr. President. We love our *Bill of Rights*. We love democracy. I agree with you that we do not export our best ideals, we export McDonald's instead of our best ideals. But these . . . these things of the past are past.

Renee looked at me with an expression saying do not say these things. And clearly I had not experienced my own country for quite some time or would not have purported such nonsense. It was a childlike desire on my part to want the country of my origin to live up to some of its ideals. I continued,

—We learn and we go on. We should aim for a chicken in every pot but I have noticed that even here we miss a pot here and there like a drunk trying in vain to aim at a toilet.

—Bolivar, bullshit aside, you are writing what you see to be the truth and it happens to correspond with my views. But you stop short of implicating the United States in virtually everything you write.

—I'm aware of that.

—So then why?

—Because I'm a coward. Because like Cuba they jail traitors in my country. Because after all I am still a citizen of that country by birth.

—Now you are talking honestly.

—Yes, honestly, I do not care very much for the whole concept of sovereignty, and I am sorry to be telling this to the Protector of Sovereignty.

From her expression, Renee could not believe I was talking to her president this way.

—*Está bien.* Continue.

—I've said too much.

—On the contrary, I agree. I know that I dictate. I dictate to protect. In this way, I am not so different than your paternalistic senators and father figures who are getting ready to take over your country and tear up your precious *Bill of Rights*, which by the way is a document I admire very much, though it would not work in Cuba, especially if it served as a fake façade to let unregulated capitalism rule unopposed.

He was probably right. He and Che had spent long nights together in Mexico City planning the revolution. They considered the past. When little countries like Guatemala in 1898 and 1954 tried to democratize and nationalize their interests, the U.S. Marines (or, in '54, the CIA) arrived and changed the blossoming hope of self determination back into a suitable tyranny, one that answered to Washington and Wall Street. But I was curious about his take on the current political atmosphere back home. This shift to paternal power was already taking place under Ronald Reagan.

—Meaning who?

—The extreme right of your country. I am a father figure of the left. Your new challenge will be from the right. It's classic and something tells me that you can't see it, probably because you ignore your own country. But you will stay here in Cuba, and tell the truth as you see it?

I sensed he was actually asking rather than telling, so I agreed.

—Cuba is my home now. I have Renee and the girls. Thanks to the Ministry, I have a job. I couldn't ask for more. I thank you for that.

—Renee, how is your chicken?

—It is delicious, Your Excellency.

—Bolivar, I very much admired your last article regarding the living conditions you saw in the Congo. It was intelligent and compassionate. But why do you avoid naming all of the guilty parties? You refer to them as "imperialist forces," when we both know that naming the loan sharks, Alan Greenspan and his pals, would be more to the point.

—I wrote it that way because I would someday like to visit my sister, and if I name the U.S. or any official of the U.S. in a Cuban publication, I'd be arrested at the airport.

—Damn fucking right. And you have the little girls to consider.

—Yes.

—I understand.

A look of terror struck Renee when she heard the word "arrested," but Castro didn't try to console her. The effect of his words on other people did not seem to register on him. He did say, however sarcastically,

—We will not let anything happen to our Hemingway.

Renee knew whom he meant because we had gone to visit the old man's house on our honeymoon. Everyone in our neighborhood was desperate to know how our visit with The Protector went, and Renee was very happy to oblige them with all the details. She showed everyone a picture of the three of us together, Castro in the middle looking dour and bored, and the photograph signed to the two of us and delivered a couple of days later by his own courier. I made better money now, and we moved to a larger apartment with an actual kitchen and private bathroom, in the same barrio so that Noelia would not have to change schools in the middle of her kindergarten year.

Renee settled back in to her regular work as a tour guide, and I spent a few hours a day at the office working on a book, *Four Years of Solidarity*. Most of my writing was done at home. I loathed offices. Evenings we went for long walks with the children which always ended with me carrying Noelia piggyback and Renee pushing Sophia in a stroller. On Sundays we borrowed a small fishing boat from a neighbor and fished for blue fish in the harbor, using mullets for bait. I don't think I was ever happier than then. I don't think any of us was ever happier.

When the United States dropped a biological weapon that poisoned milk and killed 27 school children, they dropped the seeds into me that grew into hatred. When they dropped sulfuric acid into Havana harbor to destroy the fishing, my hatred seethed. When they infested the tobacco crops with blue moss disease, I was tempted to write the accounts myself, but the Union editors always stopped me—Castro was keeping his promise to Renee. Protecting me did not only mean protecting me from the United States, it meant protecting me from myself. But I did write *Progression and Aggression* around then. I was ashamed of myself for doubting Castro's promise to protect me, like any other citizen of Cuba. The evening we first met, I was wary of the possibility that I might unwittingly be set up à la Jane Fonda at the antiaircraft gun in North Vietnam for propaganda purposes. Poor innocent Jane. But no. Castro kept his promise and later I vowed to myself that I would be worthy of his trust.

~ 32 ~

Vacation in Nicaragua

By the time Sophia and Noelia started calling me Popi, Renee was pregnant with Melissa. She was born on the Spring of 1986. Renee quit her job because we really didn't need the extra income as the party had been very good to us. I had turned out two decent books on Third World economic issues and the need for a Pan Latino response to U.S. aggression. Both were stamped and approved by the writer's union. If I wrote poems, I made certain that they dealt with social problems and I never made mention of any personal issues and only circulated the poems among friends and party members. There were two signs over my desk, one a quote from Bogart in *Casablanca*: "One life never made a hill of beans worth of difference in this rotten world" and the other, "A chicken for every pot."

I signed a couple of contracts to allow the books to be reprinted in Mexico City and Buenos Aires. I didn't read any reviews, but I've heard that very few readers ever made the connection between the economics work and the author of *Winter Signs*. Though books about economics might be boring and dry to some people, the books were not entirely disconnected to a novel about the slaughter of innocent Indians. It is, as Aristotle taught, the extremes of human experience we are drawn to. We had one copy of *Signs*, a gift from Fidel, but having it was I think a source of frustration for Renee until a Spanish version became available. Renee had no real interest or reason to learn English.

In 1979 war broke out in Nicaragua between the popular and legitimately elected government and the FDN (the so-called Nicaraguan Democratic Front, better known as the "Contras"). When Reagan took the White House in 1980, he rushed in like the cavalry in one of his stupid movies. In 1987, the year our daughter Melissa was born, Cuba and the United States were increasing their level of support exponentially.

It was around then that Castro sent one of his aids to my office for a quiet conversation. By this time, Renee and I had shared several dinners with Fidel. I had come to regard these dinners as pleasant intellectual exchanges, though in truth they were more like inquisitions—Castro was by nature a curious man, however stern and humorless. Sending his aid meant something official in nature, otherwise he would have simply called.

His name was Eduardo. Eduardo was a small and overly apologetic man who dressed in a suit even on hot days and sported a thin Oxford tie, not even unbuttoning his top button.

He seemed a sycophant, as his manner was so self-deprecating for someone on a mission for Castro, but then too, I often failed to realize the degree to which my own fame sometimes humbled others.

—Please, please. Make yourself comfortable, Señor Eduardo. It is very hot. Wouldn't you like to take off your suit coat?
—No. No. Thank you. No.

Señor Eduardo perched on the edge of his chair on the other side of my desk. He said,

—The President considers you, sir, a very close friend.
—We are indeed. [This was quite simply a lie, as Castro really did not have any friends, including me.]
—It is for this reason that he has asked me to ask you, with the utmost

respect, for a favor, with the understanding of course that you are to feel no pressure whatsoever and that you may feel completely free to say no to his request.

—I understand. If it is something I can do, I'll do it.

—It is that . . . It is that the President sees in you someone with a great many talents, someone who might wish to volunteer your assistance with a small problem.

—Just tell me what this involves, Eduardo. Please, you need not worry. If I think I can't do it, I'll tell you so.

—The President believes that your ability with American English and your knowledge of the struggle, could be of invaluable service to the Sandinistas just now. And if you choose to help them, you will have our full support. Any sign of trouble for you and we can get you out.

—I see. Well. No, I don't see. I don't understand how my English would be of help.

—This is a secret that you must not share with anyone, not even your lovely wife—*'sta bien?*

—Of course.

—It is a matter of Cuban security.

—I understand. The President can trust me.

—The Sandinistas are picking up radio transmissions in English. They have two carriers and a partial fleet in the gulf.

—American English?

What a stupid question. Of course American English. Anyway, I figured this was Cuba's way of testing my loyalty. Countries islanded by water or by ideology (or both) never actually trust anyone. It was clearly a test. Be that as it may, I discussed the request with Renee, giving her only the details I was allowed to give, and we decided to go to Nicaragua with the assurance from Castro that they would station all of us in Managua and Corinto where it was relatively safe.

The rest of the details were filled in later. Señor Eduardo gave me a stack of how-to papers on radio operation and maps. The next day I was schooled in azimuth and given another crash course on how the U.S. military determined their targets. I was to report to the Nicaraguan authorities in two weeks.

All Renee was allowed to know was that my role was diplomatic and that it involved communications. It promised to take several months and she did not think we should be apart that long. And Melissa was only six months old at the time.

We had to hurry but in pretty short order we had closed up the apartment in Havana, loaned out our furniture, given away the fridge, given away the clothes the girls had outgrown, hauled the books from home over to my office, and finished our packing. The girls each had one suitcase and Renee and I had Melissa's things in our backpacks. I carried a satchel that contained my Cuban passport, along with a letter of introduction from Castro that I would have to present to a military official at the airport in Managua. The five of us were taken to the airport in a purple '59 Chevy. The girls were very excited about flying. Renee was simply terrified and kept asking questions about how airplanes worked and how something so heavy could fly. I answered in soothing tones but she kept asking the same questions.

After our plane landed in Managua, we took a taxi to our hotel. I bought a prepaid phone card and telephoned my sister. It was only the second time I'd spoken to her in a few years.

—Hello, Sherry.
—Bolivar? Oh my God!
—Hi.
—Oh my God! Bolivar!
—How are you?
—You jerk!

It struck me that I had not heard English spoken in several years.

—Yes. I guess I probably am.

—You guess right. Do you know what I had to put up with?

—I'm sorry, really.

—There wasn't any more space in my garage. I had to hire you a secretary to manage your affairs. I mean, did you expect me to do all this? I got kids and a job, you know. And I got a divorce.

—I'm very sorry to hear it. Really.

—They compare you to the mysterious vanishing Salinger. You drop an important book on everyone and then you up and disappear. Where are you?

—I really can't say.

—Oh. Oh anyway, there are a few things you ought to know. I hired this secretary to manage things. She's getting sixty grand a year to manage your things, but don't give me any crap about that because you need her and you can afford her.

—Okay.

—Also I had to hire a lawyer to defend you a couple of times. You do remember that you have a daughter here, right?

—It was a girl . . .

—When you got some money, they took it, but I found you a decent lawyer to run damage control, so don't worry, most of your money is shielded from them. And BOY I gotta load of them. What a couple of ROYAL and I mean ROYAL BITCHES!

—Sorry. I'm awfully sorry.

—You wrote this "Four Years" thing, and it was translated into English. The FBI showed up at my door. They were in my living room asking questions all day!

—Are they listening right now?

There was a long pause, and then she answered.

—I wouldn't know. So... where are you now?

—I can't really tell you that.

—Well, I read an article somewhere that said you are still in Cuba and that you aren't dead.

—Trust me on this. It's better not too talk too much about where I've been.

Renee looked on curiously. It was the first time she had ever heard me speaking English. It must have jarred her a little, seeing someone you love suddenly in an entirely different context. It can even be upsetting. I myself was hearing my voice as if I were no more than a faint echo.

—All that aside, you are fine ... wherever you are?

—We're all fine.

—We who?

—Oh yeah, um . . . I got married. Renee. We have three daughters.

Renee heard me say her name to my sister.

—Three?

—Well, two of them she already had. Melissa is ours. She's our third. But they are all ours. Melissa doesn't talk yet but the other two call me Popi.

—You, a father. And what then. No more catting around?

—No. Not for a long time. Not since I met Renee.

—Where?

—Where what?

—Where did you meet her? Spain? Congo? Cuba?

—Sherry, I can't tell you that.

—Why, you tell me everything . . .

— It's better not to talk about that. Anyway, my minutes on this phone card are running out. Tell everyone I said hello and I hope we'll see each other again. Tell Dad . . .

—He's dead.

—Oh.

The minutes ran out and I sat there with the phone at my ear just starring until Renee touched my shoulder.

That night I told Renee what we… what I was doing in Nicaragua, or what I thought I was doing there. The kids were asleep and Renee listened carefully, and then she began to cry, the heaving sobbing cry that tries to hold back screams. I had to tell her that my job entailed going to other locations around Managua and Corinto, but nowhere near the fighting.

—*Oye mi amor, no pasa nada.* At the first sign of any real danger, you and the girls are out of there. Fidel promised me that he will personally see to your needs if I think you and the kids will need to go home. Please, don't cry.

—Are you stupid?

—Yes, darling, very.

—I do not care for my safety. I cannot lose you. I lost Father and Grandfather, and that is enough.

—This is nonsense. You are not going to lose me.

—No, you are the one who does not understand. If Fidel has sent you, he knows the situation here is very bad. He always wants his best people when things are very bad.

Renee only used "Fidel" when we were alone. In his presence, she could never bring herself to be so informal, nor would Castro have wanted that. He liked that people were afraid of him. His prisons were full of people who tried to put their fear aside and raise a fuss. His torture victims ran into the thousands. His graveyards ranneth over.

—If Fidel has asked you to help, it is serious. Serious like Angola.

—Renee, my darling, please, I have only been asked to listen to English on a radio, to help in *La Lucha* [The Struggle] in this very small way. All the fighting is up in the north. I won't be anywhere close.

—Promise.

—Renee, you will not be proud of me if I serve Cuba even in this small way?

—You must promise.

—Yes, I promise.

—Then . . . yes, I am proud of you.

~ 33 ~

The War

The next day we found a bus to Corinto where I was to find my contact who would guide me up the mountains to meet with a Commander. For a few days and nights, Renee and I tried to relax with the girls. Evenings we drank gold tequila and danced to the tamborazos by a gazebo under crêpe paper flags. The people in Corinto were tense or anxious, but Renee and I were too much in love and too possessed by the euphoria of romance and travel to care about another reality. It was the first time Renee had ever been in a foreign country and you could see her feet not touching the ground.

We were checked into a nice hotel for tourists. It had a swimming pool for Noelia and Sophia.

—Bye Popi! [Noelia yelled, happily splashing her sister.]
—Bye Popi! [Echoed Sophia.]

Melissa managed a little drool and a smile. Renee held her close to her breast in the shallow end of the pool. That is where I left them when I went to find my contact in one of the restaurants near the enormous orange colored cathedral. I sat on the seventh stool at "La Luna" for three and something hours until a young man sat down and asked me if I had a light.

—Would you prefer matches or a lighter?

—Matches, if you don't mind.

I produced a matchbook with the number 7 written on the inside flap and he lit his cigarette and smiled.

—Let us walk together and talk as if we were old friends who are just a little bit drunk. The Contras have spies everywhere.

That was pretty easy. After walking up and down the streets and alleys of Corinto we finally came to a rusty old Toyota.

—Now we are leaving.

Driving out of Corinto, we were flagged over by several military checkpoints. The young man, whose name was Tomás, showed them our papers, and we went on.

—You will see that our men will be suspicious of you because you look like the enemy. For now, you're a secret to almost everyone. We do not want the rebels or the CIA to know you're here.

—Is your name really Tomás?

—Yes, why lie about that?

—Are you really an American?

—I suppose so. And you? You must be important.

—Not really. I am a Captain. I mostly work in intelligence.

—I am very pleased to make your acquaintance.

—It's I who am pleased, Maestro Bolivar. I read your book.

—Which?

— *Cuatro años de solidaridad/Four Years of Solidarity*... Were the major Latin powers to maintain a four-year boycott of American products, Goliath's knees would buckle. It's that simple.

—And this is what this what this war is about. Still, I will believe it when it happens.

—I know.

—So, why are you here?

—Why are you?

—Because it is my country.

—But your cause does not know any boundaries.

—This is true.

We drove for hours in a northernly direction.

—Tomás, I am glad to know you.

—We are here. Now we are going by horseback.

A boy of about the age of one of Picasso's models was by the side of the road, holding the reigns of two horses, both of them black. Tomás told me to get on and gave me a foot up. He got on the other and the horses took us up and into the hills and into the middle of night.

The mountains were cold at night and I was not prepared for such cold, so Tomás told me to take the blanket from the horse and use it, which I did. Then I asked him about my family.

—The Colonel has made arrangements for them to be moved to a more secure place in the town.

—How close are we to the fighting from here?

—You're in it. Most of the heavy fighting is farther north on the Honduran border, but the fighting is everywhere.

My heart sank. I wanted to turn back, but only the dark horse knew what direction we'd go.

~ 34 ~

The Colonel

The Colonel came out of his tent and shook my hand. He said,

—I think you have a letter for me.
—Oh, yes.

I quickly reached for my satchel and three guns swirled around to point at my heart.

—Put them down. [He said, meaning the guns.] Just hand your satchel to Tomás, okay?

They found the letter from Fidel and the Colonel read it and handed it to a man standing a few feet behind him.

—Let's get into the tent out of the dampness.

We each sat down on a couple of wooden stools. He lit his little pipe. I was surprised to see that he was a balding, very white, blue-eyed Nicaraguan. He exhaled . . .

—You are a fucking gringo.

—No sir, I am a fucking gringo at your service.

He laughed.

—Yes, all right.

—I'm guessing that if you are listening in on transmissions in English, then they are listening to you, and, if so, you should not be using Spanish for communications. You should probably be using an indigenous dialect.

—Do you really think we are so stupid? We are a people with 10,000 years of knowing about such things.

—I apologize. You have already taken precautions.

—It doesn't matter; your CIA can quickly pin down our locations. They are not getting everything they want, but they can find the communicators.

The Colonel took out an American communications manual and handed it to Bolivar.

—I want you to learn this. We took it off a dead CIA.

—How do you know it isn't bogus, a plant?

—The circumstances. We think it's real. Read it. I think it has the codes for their frequencies. If it does, then we're going to have you have some polite conversations with a few of their pilots. They raid us daily with goddamned Apaches.

Then he showed me a map of the area and a town located at its center. We were somewhere in the middle of the northern most jungle mountains not far from the Honduran border, close to where the Contras maintained their central command. On the map lay a little town called Zelaya, which the Colonel kept jabbing at with a wooden pointer.

—We are five kilometers from this town. It is being attacked almost every day.

He pointed to more places on the map.

—These are all hot, but we control them. You'll be given your orders. If you are not clear about them, you need to say so. Do you understand?

—Yes.

—I will not lie to you. The job you signed up for is dangerous. I will pray to God for your safety. And for your family.

I did not say it but I could not help noticing that a communist had just invoked the Lord. The longer I was in Latin America, the less befuddled I was by contradictions.

The Colonel re-lit his pipe, puffed once, and said,

—This isn't like other wars you've read about. It isn't like your Vietnam. We have already taken many times your casualties in that war. We're getting close to around three million. That's your Vietnam times thirty-eight.

The Colonel was right. President Reagan was really racking up the bodies, and for what? The notion that opposing economic views—public things should be private or private things should be public—seemed a paltry dilemma in the face of so much killing. And all of this was going unnoticed. There were whispers and leaks; there was the Iran-Contra business; but hardly any Americans even knew the U.S. was running combat missions daily. Most Americans were busy watching movies about successful Wall Street brokers and trying to get rich in the dot-com bubble. The former anti-war hippies were even leading the charge of capitalism. The familiar adage was "Greed is good."

I listened to the Colonel explain the situation for a long time. When he finished, it was dark. There at the end of his talk he suddenly changed his topic.

—I very much liked your book.
—Which one?
—*Las Señales del Invierno*. I also admire the books of Zane Grey.
—You should be praised for the inclusivity of your literary taste, but I have to say, I am a little uncomfortable in the company of the great Zane Grey and the Cowboys and Indians genre.
—Tomás will finish your briefing. I am pleased that you are here. Did you really know Señor Bland?
—Yes, Colonel, I knew him.

The Colonel me patted my shoulder and said,

—I'm very glad you are with us.

He motioned to Tomás to escort me to my tent.
For the following days I studied the manual and received briefings from Tomás. We were fairly certain we had figured out the codes that unraveled their frequencies. Then, about a week had passed when Tomás appeared with a new map and a field radio. He pointed to three locations where I could travel by horse to listen. He also gave me a list of locations to feed them so that they would either hit bare ground, U.S. Special Forces, or allied Contras. Just stick my voice out there and tell them to hit such and such hilltop . . . with such and such coordinates. When the briefings finished he took me to another tent stored with ordinance and weapons. Tomás motioned to me and said,

—Take whatever.
—Tomás. I haven't the foggiest idea how to use any of these things.

—We will train you tomorrow. For now, just choose a weapon.

—I really don't think I need one.

—It is better if you chose, or I am directed to make the choice.

—Very well then. You tell me. What is the simplest little thing you have?

Tomás picked up a rifle that looked like the one I'd seen Zapata holding in photographs. The Mexican Revolution was my closest cultural reference point to Nicaragua and the cause seemed similar.

—It only holds five rounds of 45/70 and is best for short range. I think you would be better off with an A.K.

—I'll just carry this one.

—It was made in the United States to kill buffalos. Zapata himself had one very like it. Tomorrow I will show you how to use it. Oh . . . and . . . you better change into this uniform and wear this red bandana around your neck or you will likely be shot by one of us. I'm sorry that the uniform is only that of a private's, but we think you'll be safer that way. If you come across a superior, just produce your orders and he'll let you pass.

~ 35 ~

Azimuth and the Perversion of Symbolic Logic

The following day, I was trained by a Lieutenant Chucho for 20 minutes on the rifle. I'd already been schooled about the map and radio back in Havana. Tomás gave me a horse, some provisions and a compass, and told me to travel to the top of Point "X." The long Indian names for the hills around here were renamed for me on the map, replaced with simple letters. I had the cipher for their frequencies. A canteen, the water, provisions, my compass and map were stuffed into a saddlebag. There was a great deal of movement in the camp, men cleaning and checking their weapons, taking down tents.

My secondary points were "Y" and "Z," which made me wish I had paid more attention in those classes on symbolic geometry, where the final letters of language were as respected as much as a soul's last breath.

I walked the horse through much of the route, checking the topo every few hundred yards against my map and the hilltop I'd chosen to line up with. The jungle was quite a bit colder than the Congo, but like all jungles it was a shroud over time and distance and I could not help but remember the images of Marie Ella and watch her dance across the stage in the back of my mind, wondering if she were alive somewhere, if she and her child were living.

I was alone on the top of X. Deal with it, Descartes. After three days of listening to our ground troop communiqués in Spanish, I picked up one in English, chopper wings in the background. I had locked on to his frequency.

— This is Tail Feather. Going in.

The pilot confirmed his strike code, and when he did I quickly jumped on the microphone. Scanning the list for the most probable location of Contras, I told him to abort his coordinates and lock on to the new ones. Before my command could be countered, it was over. I could hear the pilots arguing as to what had just happened. I could hear Tail Feather getting yelled at and being ordered to return to the carrier. I had to move now. "They can find our communications pretty quickly," the Colonel had said.

In that moment I did not know if I had saved any lives or taken dozens. I'd never know.

The next day the fighting intensified over the airwaves, and I got a direct message in frenzied Spanish, using my own name: Bolivar, move to Z, skip Y, and move directly to Z. So much for logic. War is a series of non sequiturs. Z was actually one of the several hills surrounding the town of Zelaya.

I arrived at Z. Z was a smoldering crater on the top of a hill. I got back on my horse and rode down and up to the next ridge, riding right into my comrades who were as about as freaked out to see me as I was to see them. And I was lucky they didn't shoot me on sight. When their Sergeant, a girl who couldn't have been more than 16, had sorted out my orders, she told me to go with the others into Zelaya and hold any high point I could find. She left me with a note of caution that CIA and Contras were dressing like us to break our lines. She said,

—As for that, as far as I know you could be CIA.

The highest point I could find was one of the bell towers of the enormous orange cathedral like the one in Corinto where I had shown Renee how people kneel and pray only a few weeks before. She was curious but skeptical. Later we danced under the Tule trees to the music from the tamborazos in the square, an activity she likened to her version of religion.

I leaned Zapata's gun against the stone. Exhausted, I took off my boots and my socks. In one of my socks I dropped in three bullets for good luck, one for the Father, the Son, and the Holy Ghost. Amen. I tied the sock, tied the boots together, and rested my head on the boots. I don't know how long I was asleep. Gunfire and bright flashes from flares awakened me. I slid my ammunition sock into my left pocket and slipped on my boots. Then I peered out at the city around me.

A third of the houses and buildings were demolished by bombs. I could also see American made tanks perched on the hills on three corners surrounding the town. There was a sudden scream of air, a sound I remembered from Africa, fighter jets swooping down to strafe the city. They were F16s and they left vapor trails as they shot back out of their dives and tilted east into the sun, toward their aircraft carrier somewhere in the Gulf of Mexico. I thought about food and wanted to sleep and maybe I prayed. If I did, the prayer was interrupted.

The helicopter hovered so close that I could see the pilot. He looked more like a fly than a man. With bulbous black sunglasses, I took him for a fly. I didn't think. I just aimed and fired. Through my sites I saw his head fling backward and now the co-pilot fumbling for control. The Apache spun around the way maple leaf wings twirl and fall. It crashed into the gazebo, exploding and sending large pieces of metal and mushrooms of fire into the Tule trees in the town's square.

Then over the hills that surround Zelaya, I counted three more helicopters on the horizon. They drew my attention away from the tank on the northeast corner of the plaza and the Contras taking up positions along the pillars of the town's center and arcade. More helicopters—Apaches. You think of the strangest things. I accidentally stirred up a family of red hornets in a sand box on the family farm. I was about Sophia's age . . . I was dragging a toy tractor and plough through the sand, getting the sand, the earth, ready for the winter freeze. After several direct hits, my grandmother brought out a gallon of red diesel to douse the sand box. Then she drove me to the hospital.

In a few seconds that seemed like forever in a memory, another one hovered. It only occurred to me later that the fly was a man, the fly and his crew were men . . . maybe from Kansas or Missouri. In my dreams I jumped out of the tower before the tank shell or whatever it was blew the tower apart, and I landed hard against the flagstone tile roof between the weeds that were growing there and rolled head over feet off the cathedral until the bones in my body crashed some fifty feet below.

~ 36 ~

Teodesia

We are overrun. It feels like a rush. This, the enemy, my friend, the morphine and blue lights of the bunker. I know the shells are not the sea shells peacefully drifting up on the shore. They are exploding in waves all around us and in the midst of blue dust drifting down through the blue Christmas lights strung up in the bunker of whistles and screams, flashes of light affixing a moment on a nurse, covered in my blood, or the guy who is screaming next to me, as she squats, crouches, aiming a 45 up the stairs that ascend upward into the face of the enemy. Zips in the wire. Strange word, "zips." "Zips in the wire," someone is screaming. Do you want to unzip me? Here? Now? In the middle of this dream? Blue Jacket has come to warn of a possible attack from the Sioux, the North Vietnamese Sioux. He is disguised, wearing the uniform of the Union. The cavalry will intervene. Ronald Reagan in black and white will get on his horse and lead the charge, saving the Konzas and Ottawas from another vicious attack. They're all around us now, the horses, flying horses.

Suddenly, there was a woman's voice:

—Salazar says you are going to be fine but keep your mouth shut when you dream and don't speak English.

—Who is Salazar?

In my dreams I jumped from the tower. But that is not how it happened. There was a feeling of impact and I remember flying. I remember flagstone or slate roof tiles and sprouts of weeds and flying. Other things I am not sure about, but a nurse has pieced the event together, planting memories that I am not sure are my own. I think I dreamed pieces of a story Yarnie had told me.

It was a baseless and instinctual guilt that made me wonder if Yarnie would forgive me for confusing myself with him. Probably he would. He and a buddy once fragged one of their own, a second lieutenant after one too many bad orders. They were taking fire when they did it . . . just tossed two grenades in his lap and then went right back to return fire on the North Vietnamese. Yarnie said his platoon never knew, but no one was sorry. No remorse. Yarnie said,

—No remorse, Bolivar. That's the horror. I still have no remorse. But the replacement wasn't any better and he was killed the next day and replaced with a decent, common sense sergeant who managed to keep most of us alive for another few months before Tet. They're all still back there. Sometimes I dream that one of them is calling me, holding up my middle finger and telling me to come back and get it.

When I regained consciousness, the first words were from a nurse. I learned her name was Teodesia. She said,

—We held the town for a week. You are hurt very badly.

I tried to move.

—You will not be able to move for quite some time. A doctor will be here to explain to you.
—Renee . . .
—You have spoken about her often. Is she your wife?

—Yes. Please I . . .

I lost consciousness again. According to Dr. Salazar, who wasn't sure whose side I was on, I had simply fallen from some height, which I must have done since I wasn't found in the bell tower, but on top of another man. Both of us were taken for dead, but out of dumb luck, the man I fell on, who was already dead when I fell on him, broke my fall. Salazar had a removed some of his splintered ribs from my side. My other side was also cut deeply by a shard of rock or shrapnel from the tank that blew the bell tower off the cathedral. A couple of men from Tomás' group recognized me when they were pulling the dead into the church. When they came to pull me off the dead man who cushioned my fall, blood and air gurgled and frothed out of my left lung and through a hole in my chest. Then they realized I was alive and grouped me with their own wounded.

I regained consciousness again and Teodesia's face came into view, only I didn't know her name then.

—¡Hola! Oye hombre, tienes que cuidar lo que dices cuando estás dormido. [She whispered.] Be careful what you say when you're asleep. You don't want Salazar to hear some of the things you have been muttering, which is in very fine Spanish, but not always in Spanish. We aren't sure about Salazar's allegiances—okay? I take it you are not from here. Where are you from?

—I think I better not say just now.

—No, maybe you shouldn't. Well, you've broken both of your legs. One in three places. You shattered your right arm, punctured a lung, suffered a nasty blow to the head, you were hit I think by shrapnel, and most of your ribs are broken. Also your pelvic bone is broken. In short you are pretty lucky to be alive.

—I want to go. I want you to find my family.

—I have already done some asking. There is a letter. I think it is from your wife. I'm sure she is fine.

—I have children.

—I am sure they are fine too. I have the letter. I have not opened it. I will slip it under your pillow and when you are able, you can read it yourself.

—No. No, please open it and tell me what it says.

—Are you sure?

—First, tell me if we won.

—We fought for over a week. We held this town. In a way, that is a victory. But now the Contras are back.

—Should I read this?

—Yes.

Teodesia carefully opened the letter and started to read it out loud.

—Estimado Collins, it is with a terrible sorrow . . .

Teodesia's lips moved a little more, but she was not saying the words. Then she slumped forward.

—Oh, *Señor.* No. This is not something I can tell you.

—Please try. It's from my commander, Colonel Aguilar—yes?

—No. No. It's from the President . . . It says,

> Estimado Collins,
>   It is with a terrible sorrow that I bear this news to you that your wife, Renee, and your three daughters, were killed by an American bomb. This occurred on November 6th, 1988, in Corinto. We can say with certainty that they did not suffer. We can also say that your wife and daughters are very proud of you for your service. For your service and sacrifice, Nicaragua also honors you. Your condition has come to my attention, but while you are a hero, it is safer for you that we do not make your story public. However, I will personally make sure that President Castro hears of this on your

behalf. Words cannot convey how truly sorry we
are for your loss.

Signed,

Daniel Ortega
President of Nicaragua

—There is something else. It is a medal of some sort.

Teodesia folded the letter and gently put it back into its envelope. She
slipped the letter and the medal deeply inside my boot.

—Better to keep this close to you.

Her eyes were rimmed with tears and she lowered her head and said only,

—You better rest now.

> It was a village in the south, remember?
> Life was quiet.
> Days spent in the yard of the ruined church.
> Grass curving away from the stone fragments.
> Processionals of ivy
> and the palomas crooned in consolation the
>   palimpsest
> of now and then,
> and the signs went undivined in his "labyrinth of
>   solitude"—
> It's true, then.
> There are no open doors.

The Nowhere Man

It was from the village
my letters took weeks to reach the afterlife.

Here and there,
tanks, machine guns, the brown boys in their
    flak jackets
and Teflon helmets
posed in the corners of the square
or peered from the bell towers
like visitors to the nativity.

You stayed awhile with me, didn't you?
under the parasols of palm and Tule
and your shade and mine joined
and was called the night of faith,
night everlasting.

Leaves shuffled.
Colored lights illumined the crêpe paper flags,
and we danced to the tamborazos till you
    disappeared.

Then a fire rained
and for the next few thousand years
it finally dawned,
this emptiness.

Nights the rain came through the broken windows
and soaked the bed.
A poor rat scurried under the chair to dry off.

I wrote there the long letters on torn,
brown paper bags,
seeing the words flicker in candlelight—
each said love . . . love . . .
Or once,
"we have taken the town."
Somewhere over the dark, green hills,
a river carried away the naked body
*   of our love.*

It couldn't last.
We had taken the message so far.
I couldn't say anymore what you looked like.
I couldn't remember my own face
after the bombs had shattered the mirrors.
I tried to turn the blood to wine, and the wine
to words
to write to you just once more,
but in all this madness
I took to dancing and danced under the trees so
*   long*
the wind and rain in their limbs became your
*   voice.*

~ 37 ~

The End of Philosophy

—How are you feeling today?

—I am all right. You know, you don't have a Nicaraguan accent.

—That is because I am from México. And you will not need to be in traction any longer.

Teodesia had a male assistant with her to help her remove the contraptions. His name tag said "Bernardo."

—How long have I been here now?

—About two months. You are healing fast, considering.

When Bernardo left, Teodesia leaned over and said,

—I have spoken with Dr. Salazar, the doctor who did most of the work on you, including the wound to your chest, which was the most serious. Anyway, he has agreed to report that you were in a car accident. We don't want a Contra spy to know that Bolivar Collins is in Nicaragua. Also, we've changed the names on your papers to Lawrence Woodsen. You're a member of the International Red Cross and you are from England. Can you sound like you are English?

—A car accident? An English accent?

—That's right. Just for now, until we can get you safely out of the country. A car accident. It's believable because there were so many people in a panic to leave Zelaya. Anyway there is a rumor floating around that you singlehandedly took down an American helicopter. There is also a rumor that someone with a flawless American accent gave out fake orders during the battle. And if these rumors spread, the Contras will infiltrate, which doesn't just put you in danger. Salazar is sympathetic but he doesn't want anything to do with either side. He knows your wounds are from fighting, but I persuaded him.

—Okay. A car. I don't really care what happens to me.

—No. I understand that. But I care, okay? So do it for me. Haven't I been good to you? You'll agree it was a car accident.

—All right. Yes. But aren't you in over your head? And what is a nice Méxican girl doing mixed up in all of this?

She ignored my question.

—We are going to take off your casts in a couple of weeks. You'll be starting a program of physical therapy. Here, I brought you something.

Teodesia produced a little box decorated with a Miskito ribbon.

—I can't . . .

—I will open it for you. I made it. I hope you like it. Think of it as something like a rosary, only a rosary from nature. You see, it is a necklace made from cloves. You soften them in water for a couple of days and then sew them together. It's simple.

—Thank you.

—No, it's nothing.

—Will you put it in my hand?

She laid the clove rosary in my hand.

—Now, all we need is a cross.
—I thought maybe you didn't believe in God, but I will find you a cross for your necklace.
—I don't know what I believe. I was beginning to think I believed in something. I don't know what I believe. Thank you for this, Teodesia. May I call you Teodesia?
—That is my name, so why not?
—What is your whole name?
—Teodesia Segovia Licea.
—Licea is a French name.
—Some ancestor was French, but nobody remembers that far back.

I thought to myself, *Yes, the Revolution erased virtually everyone's history.* Now history is busy erasing all traces of the "little conflicts in Latin America."

With canes I was able to walk reasonably well after five months, so I asked Teodesia to help me find my family's graves, which meant she would have to go with me to Corinto. Their bodies were buried with a great many others behind a small red and white church on one of the four hills overlooking the city. Their names were registered by the priest who prayed for them and presided over the burial. His name was Father Ernesto, and Teodesia had sent word that we were coming. Father Ernesto was a very gentle man. He greeted me with a smile and a look of sympathy.

—You are Sr. Woodsen from England? I was very sorry to hear about your car accident. More sorry to know of your loss. It was a dignified ceremony. A young man named Tomás was able to identify them properly. Here, this way. They are here.

There were rows and rows of small white crosses, each numbered, some with flowers and candles burning beside them. Teodesia held my flowers for me as I was still using two canes. Father Ernesto shook his head. He pulled an envelope out of his pocket and handed it to Teodesia. There was a number written on the outside. Inside was Renee's wedding ring.

—It is hard to believe that it has been five months already. Would you like me to say a prayer with you, or would you prefer to be left alone now?
—A prayer would be nice, Father.

Teodesia and Father Ernesto bowed their heads and I looked down at the little crosses wondering which was Renee's, which Melissa's, Noelia's, and Sophia's. When he finished, he slipped a piece of paper into Teodesia's fingers. It matched the numbers on the crosses to the bodies beneath them. She lay the flowers down.

—Would you like me to arrange the flowers now?
—Yes.
—Would you like me to tell you which is which?
—Yes.

~ 38 ~

"Steve"

As Teodesia helped me navigate the steps leading down from the red and white cathedral, I held on to a metal pipe that was salvaged to make a handrail. We were half way down when I recognized a man I'd once known in what was now another lifetime. He was crossing the street at the bottom of the hill. At first I was not sure.

—What's wrong? What is it?
—Probably nothing. [I said.]

But then I saw him again when we passed the open market—"Steve"— the farm boy from Iowa. It stopped me cold in my steps. I must have turned pale because Teodesia said . . .

—You don't look so good.
—It's him. It's Steve.
—Who? What Steve?
—Steve. He is a very bad man.

He still had not seen us or perhaps he was too busy taking photographs of boys who were in the market to buy food. The CIA photographs anyone they suspect, plus anyone else, and gives the pictures to the Contras, who in turn kidnap them and take them to the jungle to execute.

—Teodesia, have there been any abductions in the last few months since I've been laid up?

—Yes, about a dozen or so every week. Contras in Sandinista uniforms pick them up in the middle of the night. No one has seen any of them or knows where they are.

—They're dead. I need you to get a message to Tomás, will you?

—What's this about?

—First, before I write to Tomás, find out what hotel that man is staying at. Have a kid tag him and find out where exactly he is staying and whether or not he changes where he stays. Don't you go looking. A child's curiosity is natural. If you go looking, you'll get yourself targeted, understand? Also, have the kid see if he notices a tattoo of an anchor on that man's right forearm.

—Yes.

—Keep your distance. And keep your distance from me until Tomás can be informed.

—How are you going to manage the rest of the way home?

—I'll manage.

I asked Teodesia to leave me on the corner. She went north, quickly. I hobbled slowly south, then went a roundabout way to avoid running into Steve face-to-face. I had to hobble and I supposed the hobble worked to my advantage, but I was white, and that is difficult for anyone to miss in Corinto, let alone a professional observer.

Teodesia slipped in the backway of my hotel around midnight and knocked on my door. I was awake, waiting.

—His name is Hans Hoffman. He is German and was allowed to enter Nicaragua because he is with the International Red Cross. He has the tattoo as you described.

—Right. Red Cross. Telephoto lens is standard issue now. I need paper. I need to write a note for Tomás.

Teodesia said that she was pretty sure who she could trust to get the note to Captain Tomás. It must have arrived the very next day, for the next night someone tossed a grenade through Steve's hotel room window sometime after three in the morning. The whole city heard the explosion. By the afternoon of the following day, the Red Cross issued a statement in response to a query from the newspaper. No Hans Hoffman from Germany in the Red Cross present in Nicaragua. Stop.

For a while the nightly abductions came to a halt. A week or so later, I was having lunch as usual with Teodesia. She said that Tomás wanted to know how I knew.

—You can just tell him that I will explain when I see him.

~ 39 ~

Mexico City

. . . no foot prints . . . no huellas . . . no reflection in the mirror . . . nothing to return to . . .

Teodesia and I returned to Zelaya together. I still had regular physical therapy to work on muscles that atrophied after so many months in bed. But I was gaining my strength. When we got back the telephones were working again in Corinto so I went to a public phone to call my sister.

—Hello?
—Sherry, it's me.
—Where now?

I didn't say anything for a moment. Then I said,

—Hope to be home soon, at least for a visit.
—Are you okay?
—There was a minor car accident, but I'm fine now.
—And the kids?
—They're fine.
—So you are living the easy life? You never told me your kid's names. I'm an aunt, if they're legit, and you never told me their names.

—I'll write to you about them.

—Tell me now.

—My wife's name is Renee. The girls are Noelia, Sophia, and Melissa. Melissa is . . . almost one.

I think I could not tell my sister because their deaths were not yet real to me.

—Pretty names.

—Anything I should know? Is that secretary person still taking care of things?

—You've gone through several. But yes, you have help. Do you need anything?

—Actually I could use a little money. I have the matter of a little hospital bill here. Nothing serious.

I gave Sherry the name of a local bank, account and routing information, and told her how much to send. I had her send the money to Teodesia and asked her not to mention the transaction to anyone. It was not enough money to draw anyone's attention.

—Okay, I'll pass this along. You should see it probably on Monday or Tuesday.

—I appreciate it. I know that I've never done anything for you. I've never been there for you. I want you to know that I am sorry, and someday I will find a way to make it up to you.

—Whatever. You sound different, Bolivar. You sure you are okay?

—I miss . . . I miss things.

—Your family?

—How is our brother?

—The same.

—Still a professor?

—An associate professor! He just made tenure.

—He was always the smart one.

—Why don't you ever call him?

—I guess . . . because. Oh, Sherry, I don't know. I guess I just let too much time go by.

—Never too late little brother.

—Maybe not. I'll write first. I should have an address soon.

—Do that.

—My minutes are about up.

—Bye, dear.

The time ran out before I could say goodbye. It wasn't safe in Zelaya. It wasn't safe anywhere in Nicaragua. Those who could leave, did leave. The fighting continued in the hills, and I contacted Tomás to see if I could help. But he said that I would not be able to keep up with them due to my wounds. He said I would be safer if I went back to Havana. He said he could arrange it.

—I was thinking maybe México City. I'd blend in better there. I haven't anything to go back to in Havana.

That night I took Teodesia to dinner at a modest restaurant. On a lark, I winged it with just one cane. The right leg, that sustained the three breaks, was the more difficult to manage. By then we had become good friends. I confided many things to her. Eventually I told her that I was an American, which she already knew, but hadn't heard me confirm or deny anything. I told her all about the children, and Renee, how I had left New York after going to school there, some of the places I went, Africa, then living in Cuba, up to the present time. And she told me things too. Her father was a drunk and a macho, and she and her siblings were glad to be rid of him. She lived with her mother and two of her sisters who weren't married yet. One of her brothers was killed the same day I flew out of the bell tower, surrounded by the hornets of childhood. She was in Nicaragua because her mother left her husband in México to be with a Nicaraguan man, and she took the kids with her. That's how Teodesia's brother ended up in the Nicaraguan army. Gradually, Teodesia had become more political. As it turns out, she knew Tomás in High School, and liked him, so it was fairly easy for Tomás to count on her to be an informant for him when Ortega came to power.

—Do you think you'll stay? [I asked her.]

—For a while. I still miss México. I grew up in a small town called Jlalpan. And you? What are you going to do? Go back to Cuba?

—Not Cuba. Cuba died with Renee and the girls. I'm not sure I have a home now. I am going to find a place in Mexico City. I'd like for you to visit me, if you can.

—It's pretty far.

—I know.

—Perhaps I may. I have only been there once. When I was very little, my father took us to see the city. I still have grandparents in Jlalpan. I will write to them and you can go to see them.

—I would like that.

—Where are you going to stay in Mexico?

—I'll have to write to you. I don't yet know. Teodesia, you have been a very good friend to me. I want you to know that I appreciate what you've done.

—I know. But you are the hero, Señor Bolivar.

She said that in a funny, teasing way. We laughed. I ordered two more beers—Pacificos.

—Why aren't you married? You are very pretty.

She shrugged, embarrassed, and looked away.

—A "brindis!" This drink is for the lovely Teodesia.

She became serious.

—You believe that you will never love again, but you will.
—No. I won't.

I thought that I would blend in, in Mexico City, as just another foreigner. There were Dutch, French, Spanish, Japanese, Americans. The whole rest of the world was in Mexico City.

I found an apartment on the Avenue of Mysteries. Most days I stayed in and wrote. I began to write another novel, *Vivaldi's Lovers*, and it was going quite badly. Some weeks not at all. On Sundays I wandered around the flea market at La Lagunilla on the edge of the Tepito district. At times, I began to long for company but I did not give into these longings. Occasionally I went to the Condesa, where there are nice restaurants. The Condesa is something of the bohemian area—at least that is what people like to think, and a number of not so bad writers and artists live there. Sometimes I enjoyed the company of poets who lived in the neighborhood. Mostly I liked the restaurants and the trees, so I went there to pass the evenings.

~ 40 ~

A Letter to Renee

I often wrote about them when they were alive, when Cuba islanded my life and lulled me into a sense of contentment and happiness. Mostly they were love poems for Renee, vignettes about Noelia and Sophia and the baby. Sometimes I wrote detailed plans and drew sketches for the little farm we had requested—such things had been made possible under Leninist economics, the small but private ownership of farms. I was working on that the day that Fidel sent his request in the person of Eduardo. Not since we'd all gone to Nicaragua had I loved them in words. I had not written a word about Renee or the children. I couldn't make any sense of it and I still can't. But three years after her death, I did try to say something to her. I do not know if people can hear us from the beyond:

It's Sunday morning. I don't know if this letter will find you and the children, or even if I'll ever find my own footprints again, or what it was I was searching for. Maybe now my letter to you is simply a pre-ontological echo in the immensity. This morning I walked out into the noise of everything—alarms, vulgarities, trumpets. A man was playing an old violin where I wandered among tiendas. He played only the same few notes, so few I imagined I could hold them in my hand, like Beethoven's A and B in the 15th Quartet in A Minor, after he had gone completely deaf.

Oh Renee, there are too many things . . . blunderbusses, puffer fish, funerary pots, samurai swords, and yellowed lace. There is an iron bird cage, a medieval-looking thing said to have held the head of General José María Morelos y Pavón. There is a lady's kerchief, bearing somewhere in the corner a hieroglyph, a sign, my lost letters and diaries. There are glass negatives of the dead staring back at me from yellow and brown clouds when you hold them up to the light, their minds translucent and empty.

This is where I look for you on Sunday mornings, among a supernumerous profusion of used and useless wares, of which I too am part. The gynecologist from Pakistan, an immigrant who died here in Mexico and left the records of a thousand women, left me here too, in one of his pinewood drawers, the one marked "negatives," by the one with carved whale teeth, and the one with Nazi insignia, colored stones and glass, scorpions woven from vanilla twigs. There's a drawer for everything and everyone. That means you too, I guess.

We get so mixed up and turned around until we wake up, if we ever wake up, dreaming we ARE that mythological creature in the mirror, the loose assemblage of odd parts, bricolage, amputee, alebrije—deer foot/fox head/monkey hands/beak mouth . . . and we run away in terror, run until the crosses bleed real blood.

I tried to remember all of our nights, the oil lamp, your soft skin, and the books sewn from lambs. Now I read. I read for much of the night. On Sundays I come here to look for you. Today I bought an old blue bottle because I believe it contains a night, your sugarcaned breath still lingering in the bottle.

I wrote to Renee in English. I imagine that if souls can hear us, they probably do not hear us in any particular language, or they can hear us in all of them.

~ 41 ~

Vivaldi's Lovers

When the war began to wind down two years later, Teodesia made good on her promise to visit me. I was still working, slowly, on the second novel. It was going nowhere. I spent more time at restaurants in the Condesa, sometimes with Chumacero, sometimes with Mastretta—local writers.

This Vivaldi thing. I do not know how it occurred to me, or why years had passed before I sat down and started to write it. I remember a conversation in Havana with a well-educated elderly Cuban lady named Beatrice. I met her one afternoon when I was watching the kids play in the park. She mused on and on about Vivaldi and all of his affairs with a wry look on her face. He was one of the world's great lovers. But as I never included even the smallest sexual innuendo in *Signs,* I wondered if I could write about the man's sex life, without actually referring to sex. As for my own life, outside of my diaries, I have never spoken of such private matters, nor would I. That would be in bad taste. The seminal moment, the moment the brain has turned a fuzzy notion into an obsession and the obsession into a mad dash must have germinated sometime during Teodesia's visit to Mexico City. By this time, I became aware of the rumors in the press about my "wild life," or—how did one journalist put it?—"my infantile sexuality." It seems that Kay Sansouci, in *Harper's,* had published a completely different account of what she considered "the facts" leading up to the birth of Marti.

She trained little Marti well in the lingo, and Marti, interviewed by a jerk, is quoted as saying,

—My father is a man. All men are breeders. My father is a breeder.

My kid all right. She had mastered the syllogism by age five. But how dare someone do that to a child! I didn't know this Kay character; would never be able to describe her; can't remember her face; only know her name from court documents. Better that way. But how dare someone teach such things to a child!

Anyway, Teodesia came to visit me and for a few weeks I think I was happy. Psychologists like to say that people who have shared a trauma tend to bond to survive. Teodesia lost her brother. I lost. Everyone lost in Nicaragua. For all I know, they're still losing. As we were walking around the zocalo, she stopped. She wanted us to go into *La Catedral* and light candles for our lost ones.

Maybe it was the period architecture, the baroque carvings of the cathedral, it's vaulting ceiling leaping out of darkness, the sudden reprieve after a long sadness just by being alongside someone like her that made me dream . . . *Teodesia* . . . *Vivaldi* . . . *love* . . . . Vivaldi never wrote about the "sublime." Kant and many other philosophers devoted hundreds of pages to it. Gustav Mahler let it drift our way in symphonies. It occurred to me that I had wasted a great deal of my life inching my way like a worm through sentences, when all one really had to do was listen to Vivaldi, or Mozart, or Bach, Beethoven, Brahms, or Mahler. They all just did it. They didn't fuss over it. They did it. And we called it genius, and then we let a few foolish critics descend on Paris and New York and forthwith dispense with the notion of genius as antiquated. Sad. What makes the philosopher, the modern philosopher, unable to love is basically his or her intellectual arrogance and lack of reverence, a state of being that is natural and normal to any child crouching in front of a peony or rubbing a dandelion on his little face to paint himself yellow for no reason at all but to be yellow. I say "his," but add "her," in order to not leave out Julia Kristeva or anyone else who wields language as if it were a weapon, or a tool for militant, depraved psychoanalytic nosey-ness. All the up-tight-stay-away-from-my-ass hyper safety-conscious bourgeoisie. Alas, my comrades will not understand, nor will my countrymen understand, nor will the philosophers ever understand.

But the composers! They knew in a way that few of us can. By a miracle, they never forgot their own mortality. We stand alone in a clearing. We face a sea, a desert, the impossible, vast distances across desolate space and time, and if we are lucky, for a brief moment, that infinity rears back and roars its breath into our souls, giving us the knowledge of our own profound limitations. Sadly, it's only through a terrible solitude that we may sense the sublime.

We lit candles and afterwards she taught me how to pray the rosary for . . . how long? Teodesia induced in me a trance or a state of hypnosis. The sound of someone's heels echoing in the cathedral clicked and said, "now wake." I was growing tired. Teodesia, sometimes lost in her thoughts, stretched on beyond me for a city block before she stopped and realized I couldn't keep up.

—Teo! [I said.] You have very strong legs and make admirable strides!

I huffed. I still waddled like a duck with my cane.

—Oh. I forgot myself again! ¡Ay! Perdóname . . .
—I am becoming an old man.

She slugged me lightly on my shoulder . . .

—You are only ten years older.
—Maybe, tal vez, but this cane has made me old, old like Borges, and

blinded by your beauty.

—Don't talk that way. You know I do not know who is this "Borges."

—He was a fascist. A good writer, but a fascist. Argentina. I've mentioned him a dozen times.

—Well I don't want to know him.

—And he was blind.

—You see very well.

—Not really.

—You see me? You just said that I was beautiful.

—Then, yes. I see quite well!

She laughed and we went on. She slowed down and I tried to keep up. There were white pigeons settling in for the night along the stone window frames and circling over *La Catedral.*

> *I will be with you,*
> *a common thing you use everyday,*
> *a brush, a necklace,*
> *the favorite stone you hold in your hand*
> *when you're afraid.*
>
> *I can't be more than this*
> *and I've grown deaf to the world*
> *like an old man whose thoughts*
> *are the white birds asleep in the stones of*
> > *cathedrals,*
> *like the emptiness inside them.*

~ 42 ~

Paco

A few months passed and Teodesia came to visit again. The day she arrived I was breathless seeing her in a white dress with its colorful embroidery, and the braids of her hair woven together with colored ribbons. In Zelaya I was accustomed to seeing her in her nurse's outfit except for a few times when she wore a modest dress. Her new clothes somehow punctuated the passage of time.

She let drop from her arm a rolled canvas wrapped in brown paper.

Seeing each other startled both of us. We embraced each other with a little awkwardness that was obvious to both of us. She smelled of almonds, mangos, and papayas, which she had probably stopped to eat. The oils in her hair smelled of jungle fumes and diesel from the long bus ride from there to here.

—So? How much have you written? It better be more than you have written to me!

It's true. I am not a very good correspondent, but I never throw away a letter that someone has written to me.

—Well, I have written some things. A few poems. Part of a story.

Nothing important.

—You look good.

—No. You look good. I look like a twice baked potato.

—A what?

—That's an American thing.

—Oh! I found a book to teach me English! I want to say a few words to you in English: X . . . qs may. Hwat dime it is?

I looked at my watch and answered her in Spanish.

—*Son las tres y media de la tarde.*

—Back to Spanish! [She whined.] Oh, why won't you speak to me in English?

—What for? For one, it isn't natural to us. For another, the only reason to learn English is to read Shakespeare or to better understand your enemy.

—You are not my enemy.

—I am by accident of birth. Apart from that I very much doubt that the angels care much for the notion of "nationalities" or, for that matter, language.

—You have not changed, have you!

—Does that make you happy?

—Immensely! Incredibly! Yes, unbelievably happy!

—Then I promise you I will never change.

I had changed. I cannot tell you what month or year, but I was not the same Bolivar who was born in St. Louis, Missouri. All the articles say, "Bolivar Collins, born in St. Louis, Missouri . . . ," etc., etc.

I remember that my mother's father once said, "We perceive in a way, when we are two, the same way we do when we are eighty-two." This was his understanding of the phenomenological continuity of consciousness. Now I prefer my grandfather's way of saying it, whereas for a long time, I could not grasp simplicity or grace.

We talked a little about Father Ernesto, how very fine a priest, how very attentive. How he was brave, too, since there was still, at that time, random sniper fire, often misdirected and most people were not venturing outdoors for fear of trigger-happy Contras. She told me that Tomás had been to see her, that they remained vigilant and the people would never give up their dignity. We talked about silly things too and argued happily about the merits of new technologies. By this time, even towns like Zelaya had a cybercafe.

—If you learned how to email we could keep in touch much better. [She complained.]

—I am a . . . how do you say . . . ? [I did not know the word for Luddite in Spanish.]

. . . "old-fashioned."

—You are too old for me then!

—Yes, that is true.

—No. It is not true.

We were talking and drinking wine, and drinking . . . until Teodesia had become a little bit drunk. Dropping her inhibitions, she announced,

—I am still your nurse!

—And I am still your patient. *Tap! Tap!* [I said, punctuating twice with my cane.]

She swiveled a little, inebriated, as was I. She seldom drank more than a single glass of anything.

—I must inspect your wound. Show me your wound. Take off your shirt, god-dam-it. Here! I will take it off, you poor comrade. My hero . . .

The Nowhere Man

My brave gringo Sandinista. My Sandinista-Zapatista . . . I kiss your scars to make you well . . .

And that is how Francisco Emilio Segovia Collins was conceived, by the kissing of scars.

—Poor scar . . . poor scar . . . There's a scar in the East where Jesus lay.

Karli's Postscript

"Then Jotham Meeker took his axe and cut a berth in the ice one and one half foot by two feet, then laid down his axe and took up his ailing infant, baptizing her in the waters of the Kansas River, saying *in the name of the Father, the Son, and the Holy Ghost* . . . so that his wife could rest easier knowing her little girl's soul would go to heaven."

I have often wondered why my father wrote that. I've wondered if that particular atrocity, performed out of a twisted devotion to God, was based on some actual event or if he imagined it. I've asked my sisters, Makeila and Marti, what they think of those lines and whether they had anything to do with our father. As for that, of the three of us I am the only one who knew him. Makeila came to see us a few times in México. Marti came too, but I think it was more out of a need she had to find answers, which I don't think she found. My father was kind to them, just as gentle with them as he was with my brother Paco and me. They were all much older than I was, except for Paco, who was only two years older.

Makeila told us stories that her mother had told her. She herself never knew the Congo; she was pure Parisian. But her mother had spoken about my father so often, that she simply decided to come and see him. Every year after that, she kept coming. Marti too, though with Marti, her visits often turned into subtle inquisitions, which my father suffered gracefully, and which tried the nerves of my mother. Marti was, I think, a graduate student in philosophy.

To Marti, he was simply "absent," as she put it once when he wasn't in the room. Makeila disagreed. There were wars and circumstances and people got lost. It wasn't as easy to find people then. In turn, I related stories I'd been told—how he'd gone back for them, how he'd eventually landed in Cuba, stories I'd heard about his daughters with Renee.

Always during these visits, my brother Paco would lock himself in his room and only come out at night to take food from the refrigerator and return to his room. He did not want to know or understand my father's life. As my mother explains, Paco was a typical adolescent—always angry. His selfishness always upset me, considering how much my father did for him, always there for him, for all of us, getting him a job in New York.

None of us, except for him, had much of a problem with our father's label as a traitor. Well, it may have annoyed my Aunt Sherry. I know it did. She comes to see us every year and always has *something* to say about it, like "who on God's green earth would agree to work for Cuba!?" But my dad always brushed it off, saying he was only helping some friends he was indebted to. I know the label hurt him, though—the word *traitor.* But it pleased us that he'd stood on principles. Anyway, except for Marti, none of us was American. Noelia, Melissa, Sophia were Cubans. Makeila was an African Parisian. Paco's big drama—if we call it what it was—was about his own ambitions. We have all supposed he renounced his father's name in order to climb some social or political ladder, a ladder that he imagined more than one that really existed. As for Marti, she was completely unconcerned about his label of "traitor." I once heard her tell my mother Teodesia that she agreed with every word of his book about economics, every word. My mother confessed that she'd never read the book.

"I married your father," she said, "not his books, and I am pretty sure that this is how he wants it, too.

Ms. Regier was an old college friend of my father's. Father contacted her to see if she could help Paco find work. She visited once here in Mexico. She even adopted one of our puppies, one I named Oracle, and she even kept the name. When she telephoned me and asked me to write something about my father, my first thought was that it is impossible to summarize a life like his—there were too many variables, too much happenstance. And about the contributions he made—or some would have me say "the damage" he did—I am not qualified to say. I am qualified to attest that he did not simply disappear on his own accord.

Yes, he did disappear, and after a year now, we do not believe we will see him again. He may have been kidnapped, which, unfortunately, is very common where we live. Some say the *Cristianos* got him—there was a "Christian" fatwa—but I don't believe that. One belief, very improbable, is that he returned to active duty service for Cuba and was somewhere in Pakistan. Most of the people in our little pueblo say that the CIA got him. It's plausible, but doubtful. When the cat dies, we always blame the CIA. Actually, that is something my father used to say, and say with authority since he was familiar with how they did things. "Some actions are not, to them, cost efficient. But killing your neighbor's cat is cost efficient because the cat might really be a spy. Their problem is, however, one of proportion." He said something like that. But what does it matter? To us, my mother and I, my sisters, he has disappeared and is missed. To me and my sisters he is our father and we know he'd be here with us if he could.

A few months after he disappeared, I found some hand written pages on his desk—these and some objects he kept in his office I packed and sent to Ms. Regier (with my mother's permission of course) in hopes that she could make sense of just one of them. I was frantic and still in shock when he had not returned—mind you—he'd just gone out for a walk, and in plain sight, and our pueblo is small. But no one saw anything. I searched through these last sentences, looking for some understanding, trying to make some kind of sense. He wrote:

> It is a curious thing, the "thing," the object
> before us . . . the *ontos* the Greeks called it,
> extending on beyond us into what we cannot

control, leaving us in vertigo. You are walking in the sand by a sea or a desert and suddenly feel yourself swept away in the undertow. You can see the dunes along the shore and see back to where you were, but all you can do is reach out. You may not be saved, but you will reach. You may weep, but no one will hear you, save perhaps God, and that remains a mystery.

Perhaps you cannot understand the waves, close and away, near and far, the inaudible drift—of change going on, both inside you and outside of you. You are without a point of reference, even to yourself, unable to see yourself in the mirror as others see you. It is at this moment you are given a choice: You may decide to love, or you will drown or become lost in a desert.

My father had decided to love. But this I already knew. He loved me, my mother and brother, my half-sisters. Yet there was, to use one of my father's words, an "inscrutable" sadness about him, as if he blamed himself for the crimes of the world. His notes went on:

While you are drifting, you are desperate to bring back the bones of the forgotten, back to the surface of knowing. But we will never know. A child who is digging in the sand by the sea tries to make edges in the sand. He is trying to make all of the disparate parts cohere in order to make one thing, a totality. It is a totality that can never be achieved, not even through literature. Suddenly the child puts down his blue shovel for just a moment, but in that moment the sea takes his shovel and he rushes to grab it but it drifts away. Then the

child is angry and hysterical. The blue sea takes
the blue shovel into a night everlasting, blue
and riptidal, shoveling back into the unknown
while the sea goes on depositing its losses on
the shore, a cycle of waves tucking quietly into
themselves.

None of this interested me at the time. I only wanted him back and
these lines seemed fatalistic and dark. I refused to listen to them. He once
told me that the power of literature lies in its capacity to assuage our personal
tragedies. He said that by writing, particularly the story about Vivaldi's lovers,
he experienced an illusory moment, like a dream, that he had found his way.
The problem was always in waking. We dream we live in a world of light,
the light is sanctity and no darkness can extinguish it. He said in Spanish
Dios los hace y ellos se juntan. What God has made into one, people think they
must tear apart and group. As my father explained, we say this is the seed
of a pea. It produces nice peas, but we should say, this is a nice dry seed, as
wrinkled as the beautiful face of an old woman. It will go on to multiply in
wisdom; it produces good food. The pea, the grand old lady in her dotage
is like Sarah in the Bible. No matter how old, she will bear fruit. And each
must have a name, must be bestowed a name, and be counted by God. And
as we multiply, so too must we know the terrible sorrow of division.

The more we allow ourselves to divide and subdivide, by age, race,
nationalities, beliefs, the farther we are from God. To name is to bless, but
after we name, we simply let it go and let it grow. He gave me my name,
Karli. I am Karli Segovia Collins.

The End

Acknowledgments

The author wishes to thank the National Endowment for the Arts for granting me the time that was required to undertake this book. I would also like to thank M.E.R., a Cuban writer for her insights that led to the seventh and final draft of this book, as well as those contributions of Christopher Ward, an officer of the United States Navy and eyewitness to events that occurred in the Gulf of Mexico and Nicaragua. I gratefully acknowledge the efforts of several friends who read this carefully: Marcia Dodson, Ancel Neuburger, and George Tormohlen. I am grateful to my wife, Francisca Esteve, for her support and advice. Thank you to those of you who suffered through the long early drafts: Melanie Branham, Mariam Fleming, Demar Regier, Joel Matthews, and Karen Barron. I'm grateful for technical advice from faculty members, veteran helicopter pilots at Kansas State University School of Aviation in Salina, Kansas. Finally, I thank a certain Captain in the United States Special Forces who asked that he not be named. Lastly, I am most grateful to my visionary publisher, Debra Di Blasi, who is still unsure whether or not I am "a spy."

About the Author

Marlon L. Fick divides his time between his home in Mexico City and his work in China. The author of four previous books, he is a recipient of the National Endowment for the Arts award in writing. Books include *El niño de Safo*, *Histerias Mínimas*, and *Selected Poems*. Fick edited and translated the anthology, *The River Is Wide/El río es ancho: Twenty Mexican Poets, a Bilingual Anthology*.